Club Nero Series - The Next Chapter - Vol 4

Vol 4

Dale v Mcfarlane

Published by Dale v Mcfarlane, 2024.

CLUB NERO SERIES - THE NEXT CHAPTER - VOL 4

First edition. April 30, 2024.

Copyright © 2024 Dale v Mcfarlane.

ISBN: 979-8223622130

Written by Dale v Mcfarlane.

Dale V Mcfarlane

Club Nero Series

The Next Chapter

Chapter 1
Prologue

MALCOLM SAT ON THE stairs of his uncle Mick's house. He wiped his nose. The house was full of family and friends for his parents' funeral. Can this day just be over now Malcolm thought . That day they came back to uncle micks for the buffet. Sam appeared at the bottom of the stairs, his best friend since nursery . He came up the stairs and handed him a plate of food. He shook his head. He wasn't hungry. Sam put his arm round Malcolm and put his head on his shoulder . Uncle Mick and Uncle George appeared.at the bottom of the stairs they looked at each other and up at Malcolm and Sam " Can you give us a minute Sam? " Uncle Mick said Sam looked at Malcolm and nodded " if you need me " Malcolm nodded again . Sam went back downstairs back into the living room where the rest of the family were .

Mick looked at George and nodded " uncle George has more room for you Malcolm. We've had a chat and if it's ok you can go stay there ` ` " Can't I decide where I want to stay? " Mick sighed as he looked at George and shrugged his shoulders ." Course not it's just " Malcolm got up and stormed into the bathroom " Let him cool down he's bound to be upset because off today "

" I'll go and talk to him " Sam says while he stands at the living room door, Mick and George nod and they go back into the kitchen. Malcolm sits on the toilet crying . All he wants is his parents to be alive and this is just one big nightmare and he will wake up any minute . He didn't want to go into care either, maybe his uncles were right to live with one of them . The door knocked " Mal " " I'm ok " Sam slid down and leaned against the door to wait till Malcolm came out . Give him time to grieve as he looks round at the door .

" Malcolm open the door please " Malcolm opened the door Sam looked up tears streaming down Malcolm's face Sam stood up Sam put his arms round Malcom Lorna Malcolm's cousin came upstairs she was older than Malcolm Lorna the Sam . " You know you can come to me whenever you need to talk ok " " Thanks Lorna " . Malcolm wiped his face with water well. I guess I better go show my face again as he and Sam went back downstairs to chat to his parents, friends and relatives .

Putting on a brave face for everyone he hated, everyone was kind though making sure Malcolm was ok and there condolences regarding his parents

MALCOLM BENT DOWN IN front of his parents grave laying the flowers on the gravestone it would have been his mum's birthday today and he thought he would visit with Darian and Cameron with the baby " Hi Mum , Dad Happy birthday Mum Darian looked at Cameron holding Philip who was now six weeks old now and doing great . " Mum , Dad meet your grandson " Malcolm looked round at Darian and Cameron. They both smiled and nodded. Cameron came over and handed Philip to Malcolm . He thought about bringing him to the grave, a silly idea Malcolm thought but he wanted to do it " This is your grandparents buddy " .

Cameron looked at Darian. He nodded his head at him. Cameron slid his arm round Darians waist while Malcolm had time to visit his parents. Darian didn't want Malcolm upset but it's what he needed to do. He thought Malcolm stood up kissing Philip's head and going over to Darian and Cameron . "Ok " Cameron asked Malcolm nodded and gave a faint smile as he looked down at Philip .

" I will be I have you guys " the three of them hugged then got into the car driving home Malcolm in the back with Philip kissing his head Darian looked at Malcolm in the mirror checking to see if he was ok since he wanted to visit his parents for there birthday he didnt want him.to be sad but understood if he needed some space .

GERAINT LOOKED OVER at Sam on his computer to do some course work while Geraint was having his Chemo which sucked big time. He was on his third dose of chemo now which they both hated now that his hair was starting to fall out Geraint reached his hand out to Sam's leg . Sam looked down and over at Geraint smiling at Sam `` You need something " " Sam put down the iPad " looking over at Geraint .

"I have a deadline " Geraint reached over to Sam , Sam swallowed what's up with him he thought " Sam it can wait " " Sorry I was giving you space " Geraint snorted, shaking his head he didn't need space he thought just Sam's presence was enough for him .

" I love you "Geraint said Sam smiled patting his leg " Same Sam reached over to kiss Geraint they bumped Jodi once the nurses noticed their interaction. She thought they were a lovely couple and were always pleasant whenever Geraint came in for his Chemo session .

JENNY IS HELPING OUT at the centre which she and Malcolm had been doing past few months today Malcolm texted he was on his way Darian would be dropping him off soon she felt sad today this will be her last shift today and going travelling around Europe then Australia what she had planned with the money that Darian gave her for the surrogacy and with it she paid off some her tuition fees and the rest on her travel plans . The Centre is busy today. She has noticed some new people come in, so has Jan but it was a good thing for the homeless and others from other backgrounds just then Malcolm arrives to help out. Jenny goes into the office to see if he's ok. He did look upset if he was ok She thought .

" my mum's birthday today " " Oh Malcolm maybe you shouldn't have come in " Malcolm shook his head he had to come in to keep his mind off stuff he thought " Philip ok " Malcolm smiled thinking of his son " " He is doing good you should come over before you leave " .

Jenny did think that it would be nice to see Philip before she leaves for Travelling. " We need more plates guys " Jan shouted into the office Malcolm got up, went into the kitchen getting more plates and bringing them out. " Jenny ok " Jan asked " she's fine, will miss her though " .

"Me to " Malcolm looked up into the Hall a few people leaving or arriving but then he noticed someone he thought he knew while he helped dish out the meals " Malcolm " Jenny thought Malcolm was a bit spaced out she tugged at his jacket he looked round " what's up " He shook his head handing the ladle to Jenny is it who he thinks it is .

" Niel " He looked up at who spoke to him good god it's Malcolm it's been years since he saw Malcolm sat on the other chair god Niel looked awful he thought his hands shook whatever happened to him " Malcolm " Malcolm smiled and nodded Neil folded his arms sitting back on the chair . Malcolm thought he looks tired and looks like he has had it bad too .

" Neil what happened " He looked at Malcolm shaking his head " What about you " Malcolm brought out his phone bringing up the picture of Darian , Cameron and Philip Neil looked at it surprised at what he saw he looked at Malcolm . " You have a family " .

" I do Neil do you have somewhere to go " " yea it's a one bedroom it does for now till i find somewhere else "

" MALCOLM COULD YOU help me with something " Chris one the other volunteers asked Malcolm got up looked round at Neil tucking into his soup then went to help Chris to the store room helping with the clothes boxes " Do you know the guy you were speaking to " Malcolm looked at Chris he nodded " A long time ago he disappeared and I wondered if he was ok " .

" at least he's here to get food right that's a step " " I know " Malcolm looks round at Neil tucking into his food it did shock him to see Neil he had wondered how he was those years ago .

AT HOME MALCOLM CHECKED on Philip who was asleep in his cot all snuggled up Lydia came into the room she smiled Malcolm looked round at her while she put Philips clothes away Cameron appeared leaning against the bedroom door " Finish your chapter " Malcolm asked going over to Cameron then Lydia disappears Cameron lays his arm round Malcolm he leans into Cameron kissing his head .He seems kinda Sad Cameron thought maybe to do with going to the grave to visit his parents. Or maybe the Centre Malcolm does get sad about that whenever he goes there

" Just about taking a break you ok " Malcolm looks up at Cameron and nods looking over at Philip " I'm gonna miss Jen when she goes " " Do you want to talk about today " .

Malcolm looks up at Cameron he goes out to the landing leaning against the landing railing Cameron watches him his hands in his pockets " I saw someone I knew from " Tears stung Malcolm's eyes he looked away Cameron came to him wiping his tears away " Niel his name is Neil Cam he didn't look good I got a shock when I saw him " .Malcolm blows out a breath looking up to the ceiling .

" Malcolm he's not your responsibility I know it's hard " " I know that " Malcolm couldn't get involved with anything that happens at the centre the ones that come in are mostly there for food or to get warm from the weather .

Cameron bent down to kiss Malcolm they hugged. Cameron was right it's not his responsibility people only need help when they ask for it " I'll run you a bath " A bath would be good Malcolm thought he did feel a bit tense and a bath will help .

MALCOLM LAY HIS HEAD against the bath closing his eyes enjoying the bubbles. He shouldn't feel guilty about the past but seeing Neil brought it all back again Malcolm wondered where he was staying, maybe he should talk to Jan about it next time .

The bathroom door cracked and Darian stood at the door Malcolm looked up at him and smiled Darian came over to him he knelt down to face him " Cameron told me " Malcolm moved closer to Darian they bumped heads Darian kissed Malcolm's temple ." Im ok Darian i just got a shock "

Darian rubbed Malcolms head Malcolm closed his eyes Darian kissed Malcolm's cheek " what can i do for you " " Being here is enough " Malcolm grinds his knight in shining armour he thought he always understands Malcolm.

Darian bent to kiss Malcolm Darians Phone beeped. He sighed and stood up. Malcolm looked at him while Darian checked his Message " Need to reply to an email talk later " Malcolm nodded then Philip started crying Cameron shouted he would get him while Malcolm lay back down on the bath closing his eyes .

DARIAN CLICKED ON THE email from Clarice Midnight he had messaged her a couple days ago regarding his cure for the symptoms he was having recently . Was he turning again and whatever it was they would deal with it he still had the potion that Clarice had given him from before .

Dear Darian

Thank you for reaching out again and congratulations on the birth of your son and thank you for the wishes Lucian is doing well Hugo is loving fatherhood.

As to the cure and the strange symptoms maybe a top up would be an idea have you had any other symptoms. When I have had to do this in the past my clients have gone onto a good healthy life .

Darian thought maybe he's imagined it but the things he's been feeling just got him worried.

GERAINT WENT TO BED when they got home from the hospital while Sam checked his text from Malcolm about Neil. He thought Sam stood in the kitchen calling Malcolm .

" Hey you ok mate " " yea just a shock Sam Geraint ok "

Sam sat at the table he heard movement from upstairs Geraint going into the bathroom " yea he's just exhausted how did Neil look "

" awful Sam i think he's using " Shit Sam thought that's not good he hoped he would get help Sam heard the toilet flush and movement again Geraint going back into the living room was he sick Sam thought .

" Mate I gotta go check on Geraint, catch up this week ok " " Sure " He was a good friend Malcolm thought and he hoped Geraint would get over his Cancer .

SAM WENT INTO THE BEDROOM Geraint in bed in his pjs hat and Sam stood at the door " sexy right " Sam sniggered, shaking his head he went over to the bed sitting beside Geraint " your always sexy to me babe " Sam reached over to kiss Geraint bumping heads .

" You hungry " Sam asked Geraint shook his head "" just a drink "
" sure i can do that for you anything else " Geraint shook his head "
Just you babe " Sam smiled going round the other side of the bed laying
beside Geraint . " Malcolm ok " Sam looked up at Geraint " Hes fine
just sounded sad he will be ok "

" understandable "

Chapter 2

Neil looked up at the drop in centre he was cold his last hot meal was 3 days ago and when he had last used Neil bit his lip thinking he is hungry and the hot water at the bed sit was a bit predictable and it did say on the leaflet a hot shower clean clothes if needed which was needed he thought he went inside . Neil looked round the place biting his lip he had the shakes from his last hit .

The volunteers were setting up a few people around which wasn't too bad he thought he went over to the staff who were serving the meals. The nice lady was there today, which was good, he thought she had been nice to him the last time Neil had gone to the centre .

MALCOLM AND JENNY LIFTED out the boxes of spare food to take into the centre with Cameron's help when they got inside the lunch rush. Jan Came into the kitchen while the others put the stuff away to help them out .

" Malcolm he's here again " Malcolm looked at Cameron then Jan they went to the door Malcolm looked out Neil was by himself at the far corner huddled into himself " Trevor spoke to him he's had a shower clean clothes the place he's in not great we're gonna see if we can get him into centerpoint "

" Good idea " Malcolm said looking out to Neil Cameron lay his arm round Malcolm's shoulder he looked up at Cameron " At least he's here getting help " Jenny's phone rang off she excused herself to take the call while Malcolm and Cameron sorted out the food bank boxes into the cupboards.

Jenny came back a few minutes later she was beaming when she came into the kitchen Malcolm looked round at her " My visa has been approved " " Jenny that's great isn't it Malcolm " Malcolm smiled it was great he thought going over to Jenny hugging her finally he thought she can start making her plans now .

" All I need to do now is book the flight now " Jenny looked at Cameron and Malcolm they nodded " When is your dad coming over Cameron " " In a couple weeks he can't wait to see Philip " .

" can I see him before I go " " course you can Jen right Cam "

Cameron lay his arm round Jenny looking at Malcolm " That would be great Jenny come round for dinner ok " Jenny nodded. It was great to see the little guy before she left. Malcolm talked about him all the time whenever she saw him. They were great parents and one day she will have a family of her own in the future .

DARIAN BUTTONED HIS shirt while Dr Carson put his stethoscope away he looked round at Darian fixing himself Dr Carson stood up picking up his bag Darian looked up at him " Darian you should come into the clinic do more tests but I do think you could be stressed " Darian huffed stressed he could eat stress for dinner he thought .

"How is Philip " " He is good and I'm not doing to much Grant "

" I can't convince you with anything, can I, Darian? " Dr Carson smiled, shaking his head, picking up his bag. Darian shrugged his shoulders, grinning " You know me, I like to keep busy " . Too busy Dr Carson thought he'd been telling Darian to slow down for years .Does he listen no but one day he will hopefully .

DR CARSON WAS LEAVING just as Cameron arrived when Dr Carson drove off. What's he doing here Cameron thought he chapped on the office door and went to Darian at his desk he looked up at Cameron coming inside he smiled getting up going over to Cameron laying his arms round Cameron's shoulders they kissed . " Hi " " Hi what was Dr Carson doing here " .

" just a quick trip " Cameron cocked his head Darian grinned he gave Cameron a quick peck on the lips " Is everything ok Darian " Darian walked round to his chair he looked up at Cameron " Yes Love nothing to worry about " the door chapped Lydia came inside with Philip Cameron went to her taking Philip from her " How has he been " Cameron asked sitting down on the couch Philip on his knee .

" Fine the story time at the library will be good I noticed passing " " I saw that we should take him Darian " Cameron looked over at Darian he nodded in agreement the door chapped Claudia appeared saw Philip going over to him gushing over him .

" I COULD JUST EAT HIM up " they all laughed Claudia holding Philip it was nice to see Darian thought watching Claudia with his son " Right I better get back to work " Claudi handed Philip back to Cameron who sat him in his career " Just so you know I can babysit anytime " Claudia grinned Malcolm , Cameron and Darian looked at each other then Claudia left to go back to work .

Cameron's phone rang his publisher calling him to excuse himself while Malcolm fussed over Philip " What do you think about a christening " Malcolm looked up at Darian it's something they haven't thought about yet Malcolm went over to Darian leaning against the table next to Darian . " Yea I don't see why not see what Cameron thinks " .

Darian touched Malcolm's knee he held Darians hand leaning over to him they kissed the door open Cameron came inside Malcolm and

Darian looking over at Cameron " Not in front of the kid " Cameron says sniggering checking on Philip " Samantha wants to do Highland fling 2 " .

Cameron looks up at Darian and Malcolm who smiles at him Malcolm looks down at Darian grinning " What did you say ' " Samantha is coming over in a couple weeks she's filming at the moment we did discuss a possible sequel before what do you think . "

" Go for it right " Malcolm comes over to Cameron slides his arm round Cameron's waist looking up at him " You are about finished your other one right I think it's a great idea right Darian "Malcolm looks over at Darian he Darian nods his agreement yes Cameron thought I think it would be a good idea he thought since he has only editing to do for his next novel and they had discussed a book about their lives he was going to start soon .

" What do you think about getting Philip christened " Darian announces again why not Cameron thought he was christened " Yea we should do it " Cameron's phone rang off again this time his dad he connected the call to his dad .

" Hey dad " " How's my grandson? Cameron snorted, knowing well his dad didn't call for a catch up. He called to ask about Philip " Hello dad he's good, we're at the club right now " .

" OK I'M SENDING YOU the flight times we arrive " " great dad we're excited and can't wait to see you " Cameron smiling over at Darian and Malcolm Darian with Philip he was such a good dad Cameron thought and he couldn't wait for his dad to see Philip too .

A COUPLE DAYS LATER Geraint's friends Lauren and Jack and his fiancé Charlene came to visit they ordered Chinese to share around Lauren thought Geraint looked better even though he had his beanie on the whole time since some his hair was falling out because the chemo Jack brought out his phone so everyone could look at new photos his son who is 2 months old Charlene's parents were looking after him tonight to let them go out .

" He's so cute " Sam said looking at Geraint he smiled and nodded " We will bring him over soon it's been a while since you saw him " .Jack said looking at Charlene Sam thought the baby was cute and looked like both his parents .

Geraint got up and went over to the kitchen for a drink. Sam watched him in case he needed him. " He is doing better right? Lauren asked Sam, looked at her and nodded " Tso more sessions " . Hopefully the last " Geraint said he hoped for just two more sessions .

Geraint sat down and Sam took his hand " We Are looking into adoption and fostering "Geraint said first Lauren looked round they did talk about it before and good for them she thought . "Have you looked into surrogacy like Malcolm did? " Sam looked at Geraint and back at the others . We have but we want to find the right person and it not be too clinical like Malcolm did with Jenny " .

" That's fair enough yea I get that I would be the same if we couldn't have kids it would be the right person " Lauren listened to them discuss the situation she agreed with Sam and Geraint regarding the surrogacy .And it has to be the right person to like they mentioned before .

AFTER A WHILE IT WAS time for them to go Sam and Geraint insisted on there friends not help with the tidy up they would do it between them Geraint pinched Sam's bottom he batted him away giggling while they tidied up Geraint wrapped his arms round Sam from the back . " You ok "Sam asked, kissing Geraint " mmm " .

GERAINT KISSED SAM'S head while he did some dishes Sam turned Geraint looked down " Geraint " Geraint looked up at Sam and smirked Sam shook his head Geraint went to unzip Sam's Jeans he giggled "You have had to much wine ".Sam giggled looking at Geraint he took Sam's hand .

" No I haven't just a quickie look I'm hard " Sam looked down at Geraint unzipping his jeans yes indeed he was hard Geraint looked up at him " that's good right " Sam bent down damn I was gonna go first Geraint thought Sam palmed Geraints cock Geraint hissed that felt good stroking him Geraint shutting his eyes .

Sam took him in his mouth Geraint held onto the sink while Sam's head bobbed up and down licking and sucking his cock and balls " Jesus that's good baby " Geraint held onto Sam's head while he sucked away and flicked a finger inside too Geraint arched up and opening his legs wider for better access .Sam sucking Geraint off Sam looked up at Geraint all flushed he loved that look Sam thought .

It didn't take long Geraint to Come he looked down at Sam grinning he stood up they kissed " Good Sam asked wiping his mouth grinning " " what do you think c'mon let's get to bed " They kissed Geraint tasting the saltiness from him he slapped Sam's bottom then taking his hand going up to bed .

A FEW DAYS LATER LAUREN came to See Geraint and Sam with a proposal that she had looked into the surrogacy side and had checked out some sites for info about it .Sam looked at Geraint then looked at Lauren it would be wonderful if she could carry there child Geraint sat forward looked at Sam and back at Lauren .

" You really want to do this " " Yes i do Geraint , Sam i want to do this for you guys look at Jenny she's been brave enough to give Malcolm Philip "

Geraint looked at Sam he was biting his lip Geraint took his hand " What do you think Sam "

I think Sam thought he loved the idea of Lauren carrying their child and it's someone they know that wants to do it for them instead of the agency they checked out that provides surrogates for couples .

" Im in " Geraint smiled squeezing Sam's hand they both looked at Lauren she was beaming " What is next then " Lauren asked looking between them at who would be the one to " Well we both discussed this whenever the chance came up two of us like Darian , cam and Malcolm did " The chance that it could be twins which would be fine by them just like Malcolm thought they were prepared to have twins or triplets .

" Ok sounds ok to me " " we had our sperm frozen before Geraint got Chemo just for precaution " Sam looks at Geraint smiling at each other the doctors had suggested for Geraint to do that before he started chemo which they did .

" Both of you " Lauren asked looking between Sam and Geraint " Yes both of us that's what Darian done that's something we can discuss another time would that be ok " That's not a problem Lauren thought unusual request from both them though something she hadn't heard of two people but since Darian and his partners did it and had Philip which was a success .

" No, I understand both of you want no problem. " Sam looked at Geraint again and back at Lauren , Geraint taking Sam's hand. That's great, Sam thought, because it's what they both want. If it's twins, that's fine and they were both grateful that Lauren had come forward to offer to be their surrogate for them. She has been a good friend with Geraint since school .

Chapter 3

Jenny looked down at Philip asleep in his cot. She smiled and thought he had grown a lot since she last saw him. She will be leaving for Europe next week, a welcome break from everything and maybe find work while travelling which she planned to do. She was excited and nervous about leaving but a new adventure awaits Jenny though and excited to visit new places and cultures .

Philip whimpered he was due a feed soon Malcolm had said there were a couple bottles ready for him Lydia appeared Jenny looked over at her " He is fine Lydia is that his bottle " Lydia looked down and back up at Jenny .

" Yes " " would you mind if i give him his bottle "

" Of course you can " After Lydia left Jenny picked up Philip taking him over to the chair Jenny tried the temperature just right then Philip did a pump Jenny giggled thanks Philip she thought .

" Right little man hungry " Jenny placed Philip's bottle in his mouth. He was a little fussy at first then started to take his bottle. Jenny patted his back and he did a burp that's good she thought and sat back on the chair to give him the rest of his bottle .

" There we are " Philip took more of his bottle which Malcolm said he would certainly like his milk " Now mister you be good for your dads ok " Philip gurgled while taking his bottle Jenny imagining giving a bottle sometime in the future of her own a tear in her eyes .

Cameron came upstairs to check how Jenny was doing he heard her voice must be talking to Philip he thought " One day your dads will let you know about me " .

Cameron stood listening to what she was saying " We will meet again in the future ok " Cameron made an appearance Jenny looked up at him standing at the door, hands in pockets smiling . Jenny got up and placed Philip back in his cot Cameron came over both looking down at him " will miss you guys' ' Cameron looked round at Jenny he lay his arm around her shoulders Jenny leaned into Cameron`` Us to' ' .

" WHAT A DAY WHERE'S my boy " Malcolm announced his arrival Jenny and Cameron looked round at him he stopped looking at the two of them what's up he thought coming over to the cot is Jenny ok Malcolm asked laying his arm round Jenny " just having a moment " it is too soon for her to leave he's gonna really miss her . Cameron's phone rang Darian For face time he connected the call and why he was face timing since he was at the club Cameron thought .

" Ciao " " Hello Jenny and Malcolm has just come home " Jenny waved and Darianb nodded his head then Cameron pointed the phone to Philip they heard him say I love you in Italian Jenny was just about to leave when Malcolm stopped her .

" You ok " " I'm fine just had a moment " Jenny's phone pinged of a text she checked if her dad had come to pick her up Malcolm walked her to the door just as Sam and Geraint arrived they went into the house Malcolm hugged Jenny before she got into the car . " Catch up before you go ok " " I will " . They hugged again Malcolm squeezing her tighter " Malcolm i cant breath " They both giggled looking at each other " You good now " " I am see you soon "

Malcolm watched Jenny get into the car she waved before her Dad drove off. He will definitely miss her. She leaves to go Travelling and hopefully one day she will come back home .

" IIS DARIAN STILL AT the club " Sam asked while Malcolm went to make the coffees " Yea him and Claudia were going over the books " Sam and Geraint looked at each other what's with those two Malcolm thought Cameron came into the kitchen " Take away ordered keep some for Darian hey guys " .

" WE HAVE NEWS " SAM looked at Geraint he nodded they both looked at Malcolm and Cameron who looked at each other " Is it your treatment " Malcolm asked " No it's something else we've had a chat about it were looking into surrogacy " wow Malcolm thought good for them he thought they would make great parents " That's great guys ",

" Lauren wants to carry our baby for us " Geraint said taking Sam's hand that's great news Malcolm thought at least it's someone they know Malcolm looked at Cameron he looked pleased for them he thought " Champagne " Cameron got up Malcolm shook his head he just sounded like Darian there for a minute he looked round at Sam and Geraint who looked tired from his Chemo

" Not for me Cameron " " Babe are you ok " Geraint took Sam's hand he should stop worrying so much he thought " I'm fine just with the meds and chemo "

After an hour Sam and Geraint left Malcolm went upstairs to check on Philip who was awake when he looked in on him Malcolm bent down to pick him up " who's a cheeky boy then " pinching Philips cheek he laid him down to change his nappy "Oh my god Philip " Cameron came into the room just as Malcolm changed his nappy yes the smell got to him to .

Malcolm's phone rang Cameron took over while Malcolm checked who it was which was his uncle Mick " Uncle Mick " "Hi you're not busy are you " Mick was in Bennets at the files checking over stuff while on the phone to Malcolm " No we were just about to make dinner everything ok " .

" yes yes how's Philip " " Good "

Mick sat at his desk and put out his cigar, pouring himself a whiskey. It's been a while since he saw Malcolm when the baby came along " Your cousin Stuart got engaged " " That's brilliant news " " about time we all thought " .

Just then Malcolm heard the Rev of an engine and looked out the window Darian arriving home he watched him get out the car and stretch " Are they having an engagement party " "Not sure yet your aunty was wondering how you were reason calling " .

Darian came inside while Malcolm sat on the stairs Cameron came out of Philips room taking him downstairs Darian looked up just as Cameron came to him Darian kissed Philips head then Cameron he looked up at Malcolm he smiled and winked at him . Darian lay his arm round Cameron's shoulder going into the lounge .

" I know it's bad I haven't seen you guys In a while in college , the club then Philip I promise we will see you guys soon , oh and Geraint's treatment seems to be going well too " " that's great Malcolm and yes we should meet up soon " .

After his call Malcolm went into the lounge Darian had Philip he stood watching their interaction. It was always great to see Darian with their child. He went over to him and they kissed and then Ingride came over with his bottle to give to Darian .

" My cousin Stuart got engaged " " That's good " Darian said looking down at Philip Malcolm went into the fridge for a bottle water leaning against the counter taking a drink " Uncle Mick was asking how Philip was I said we will meet up soon it's been a while since him and aunt Morag has seen him .

" Yeah we should do that soon " Cameron said while he was checking his computer on a couple emails Darian grunted he and Mick tolerated each other for the sake of Malcolm he hadn't forgotten the time he got shut down because of the state of his pub . But that's the past ever since he had improved the pub now thankfully . Malcolm sent a text to Sam about his cousin's engagement. He texted back his surprise since they have been together seven years and a couple kids who were four and two .

FRANK IN FRONT OF Darian he whined Darian looked down at him Darian patted the couch Frank jumped up laying his head on Darians knee Frank sniffed Philips leg Darian huffed he wanted a cuddle to . Philip did a little whine Darian put his dummy back and lifted him up putting him in his rocker. Frank lay beside Philip like he has always done his way off guarding him.he was so good with Philip and there was no jealousy from him which was good they thought .

Darian came over to Cameron who was cutting the tomatoes wrapping his arms round Cameron's waist kissing his neck Cameron giggled leaning into Darian he felt his hardness against him . " Darian Longstrome restrain yourself " Cameron batted him off he turned to look at him Darian smirked " Ti Amo " " Love you to "

" Oh what's going on here then " Malcolm says coming into the kitchen smirking Darian lays out his arm Malcolm goes to him " You ok " Malcolm asks looking at Darian " Fine cant i hug my husbands "

" Of course you can " Cameron says Lydia came into the kitchen going over to Philip picking him up to take him for his bath and bed .Good Darian thought once she got a little play time .

The three of them sat at the table while Cameron dished out the pasta Darian poured the wine Malcolm dished out the bread " Great t pasta Cam " Cameron looked round at Malcolm he smiled then came over to the table sitting on the other side .

" Question " Cameron And Malcolm looked at Darian he looked up at the two of them " Glasgow opening up a new club there ideas " Malcolm sighed sitting down his fork he reached for Darians hand looking at Cameron who shrugged his shoulders shaking his head and sighing.

" Darian not tonight it's family time right Cam " Darian looked over at Cameron who carried on eating " Malcolms right Darian let's discuss tomorrow ok " Cameron looked up at Darian taking a sip of his wine .

" sorry i know its just "

Lydia came into the kitchen getting Philips bottles from the fridge she looked round at Darian, Cameron and Malcolm chatting away " Philips settled, it didn't take him long to fall asleep " .

" Thanks Lydia see you tomorrow " " I have college till 2 then i'll be along "

Lydia left leaving the cctv on the table to Philips room it will be at least a couple hours till he wakes again after they finished dinner and tidied up Malcolm went to get his laptop Cameron stopped him normally he did some coursework after dinner before downtime and Cameron did a couple of chapters of his book .The three of them looked between each other smirking eyeing each other .

Cameron wrapped his arms round Malcolm's waist. He looked up at Cameron. They kissed Malcolm and moved nearer to Cameron. He was smiling. Darian watched their interaction kissing each other. They looked over at Darian laying out their arms for him to come to them, which he did. They all snuggled in kissing each other grinding into each other they were hard . Malcolm bent down unzipping Darians jeans looking up at him watching Malcolm then popped the button Malcolm smirked then pulling down Darians jeans popping free his cock Malcolm cocked his head he licked his lips he then stroked Darians cock he hissed Cameron licked and kissed his neck Darian groaned just as Malcolm took him in his mouth .Darian arched Cameron touched his face Darian leaning into his touch they kissed again Cameron laying his hand round Darians neck .

Darian moaned into Cameron's mouth while Malcolm still worked him with his tongue Darian then held onto Cameron `` I don't want to come yet " he banged his hand on the work top Malcolm stood up wiping his mouth smirking he moved to the couch stripping looking round at Cameron and Darian who were doing the same coming over to Malcolm on the couch . Darian and Cameron bent down to him Cameron licking his stomach while Darian bent to take him in his mouth Cameron stroked himself watching Darian give Malcolm a blow job beautiful sight to see he thought always was whenever the three of them made love .

SAM CAME ROUND THE back the house to come see Malcolm and arrange there day out he stopped he could just see from through the curtains what they were up to shit he thought standing by the tree no wonder he didn't answer the text from earlier they were having sexy time lucky them he thought is it bad that i would find it sexy watching them he and Geraint hadn't much time for that lately except for that time a few days ago . No he shouldn't ogle he thought and decided to leave and go back home he giggled into himself and got embarrassed by what he saw anyway it was up to them wherever they had sex it's their home .

DARIAN , CAMERON AND Malcolm all collapsed onto the couch after there love making all sweaty and stated Malcolm sat up looking at Darian and Cameron "Well that was rather enjoyable " Malcolm said getting up picking up his clothes " Sure was " Cameron leaned over to Darian kissed him " Mm yes " a little whimper came through on the monitor the three of them looked at each other Malcolm looked at the monitor Philip still asleep . When he was awake he thought he didn't look like it through the monitor .

Darian got up pulled on his jeans " I'll go " before he went to go upstairs he turned to the others " I'm feeling a shower " smiling then left god he's some guy Malcolm thought shaking his head Cameron kissed

Malcolm's shoulder " see you up there " then left Malcolm giggled and thought I'm not gonna get any course work done tonight giggling into himself.

GERAINT WAS IN THE lounge spread along the couch he heard the front door open that was a quick visit he thought Sam came into the lounge sat on the chair beside the couch he looked shocked Geraint thought " That was quick " " They were busy " Busy with what Geraint thought staring at Sam he then giggled " They were having sexy time " .

" Holy shit really " Sam giggled sitting beside Geraint he lay his arm round Sam's shoulder " A bit embarrassing " Geraint looked at Sam surely they had the curtains closed Sam looked at Geraint he blushed " They did have the curtains closed " Sam nodded leaning his head on Geraint's shoulder that's good at least they did have the curtains shut .

Chapter 4

Malcolm was sorting out the VIP area with drinks and nibbles while the others sorted out the rooms and bar area Sam came into the club looked round at where Malcolm was and saw him sorting out the vip area " Ahh Sam Your here could you help me " Claudia asked " Sure " Malcolm looked up just as Sam and Claudia left together to do something that's weird he thought he normally comes to see him did everything go ok earlier with Lauren he thought .

SAM HELPED CLAUDIA with a couple boxes to go into the store room while the others sorted out the rooms for later since it was non club members night people still paid for the amenities too . After Sam went to the bar to check on the drinks and cocktail specials for tonight putting the cocktail menu on the tables . " Sam " He looked round at Malcolm standing. He didn't look happy. Sam thought, " What's up? " Sam asked, looking at Malcolm, " I was gonna ask the same Geraint, ok , how did it go at the hospital ?

" Fine and yes he's ok All ok for Lauren " Malcolm came closer to Sam touching his arm Sam looked down at Malcolm s hand on his arm " Sam it'll be ok takes time ok " Sam nodded he's right and for Geraint to get better they needed him to be in remission when he stops the chemo in a couple weeks .

" I saw you guys the other night " Malcolm coughed then giggled Sam blushed oh shit Malcolm thought he had thought they had been discreet the curtains were not closed enough then . " Fuck I'm sorry we well " Sam sniggered shaking his head " it's fine what you guys do in your private time I was coming over to tell you about Lauren " Sam grinned and not tell him.about watching for a few minutes.

Malcolm lay his arm round Sam they looked at each other sniggering " Are you a bit " Sam snorted batting Malcolm away " No that's fine anyway let me get on with these " Sam shook his head carrying on what he was doing he's so cute when he's flustered Malcolm thought shaking his head .

DARIAN SAT AT HIS DESK looking at his laptop, an email from Aida and a couple photos from her trip to Switzerland with friends and a couple family members looked like she had a good time which was good. She asked Philip how he was when the door knocked Malcolm came inside. Darian looked up at him coming. In and came over to Darian giving him a peck on the cheek .

" photos from Aida in Switzerland " Malcolm leaned against Darians chair looking at her photos they looked great he thought " By the way Sam saw us the other night " Darian looked up at Malcolm he was smirking looking down at Darian " he was coming over to let us know about Lauren " .

" The curtains were closed " " not closed enough " Malcolm smirked again, cocking his head looking down at Darian .

" Then next time we make sure they are " Darian touches Malcolm's leg sliding it up to his crotch Malcolm holds Darians hand " Darian Longstrome restrain yourself " Darian smirks Malcolm bends to kiss him sliding his hand to his crotch again then Malcolm stands up Darian looking at him . " I have work to do, " Darian pouts. Malcolm shakes his head in disbelief that the man he thought Malcolm blows him a kiss before leaving Darian laughs and pretends to catch his kiss .

" I love you " Malcolm shouts leaving " love you more " Darian shouts back and sits back on his chair in his bliss with the two men he is in love with. Maybe he should talk to Sam about the other night to see if he is ok with stuff .

NATHAN LOOKS DOWN AT Philip asleep in his cot so adorable he thought looking at Olivia looking down at him to he's smitten Cameron thought just like he was with him Lydia comes into the room leaving Philips bottle for whenever he wakes up "He is adorable Cameron " " Thanks and yes he is " Nathan yawns god he must be tired Cameron thought looking at his dad it is a long flight from Australia.

" We should go get settled honey " Olivia suggests yes she is probably right Nathan thought then going downstairs they had booked an apartment in Edinburgh for their stay rather than stay with Cameron even though it's a bigger house they didn't want to overstay . Cameron's phone rang facetime with Darian he connected the call " Hello Darian " " Nathan how are you " .

" we're good, we're just leaving after a long flight and Philip is just adorable " Cameron smiles " Yes he sure is we can arrange dinner " .

" We will " .

MARCUS AND RAYMOND walk into Club Nero wow they both thought this place must be a goldmine they look at each other Marcus slides his arm through Raymond's " This place is awesome " Raymond says Marcus grins and kisses him " c'mon husband what are you having " " Mm let me think " smirking at Marcus he giggles and shakes his head they both go over to the bar and order their drinks and sit on the plush seats nice they thought comfy to .

Malcolm noticed Marcus and Raymond come into the club he couldn't belIeve it seeing them last time he saw them was at school those years ago he excused himself going over to the bar .

" Well isn't this a surprise " Marcus and Raymond looked round at Malcolm standing before them Marcus and Raymond looked at each other then back at Malcolm they both stood up the three of them hugged " it sure is you got it good here Malcolm " Malcolm nods not exactly the way they think he thought and what are they doing here .

" Things are good yea what about you guys " Marcus looked at Raymond smiling they held up their hands with their wedding rings on wow Malcolm thought they got Married that's surprising " Congratulations when " " Today and we've went legit for a while to right babe " Marcus looked at Raymond smiling at him .

Raymond says holding Marcus's knee well that's another surprise Malcolm thought good on them to " Hey congratulations on the baby front man that's amazing " " Thanks he's amazing " Malcolm brings out his phone scrolls for a photo to show them how cute they both thought .Maybe one day they would have a kid of their own when the time is right Marcus thought .

" Marcus , Raymond " They look round at Sam looking surprised to see them " They got married "Malcolm announced oh wow that's a surprise Sam thought Malcolm went round to the bar and got out champagne for them " Ah man thanks how much " On the house " .

Darian came through to the bar from the office and noticed Malcolm and Sam talking to a couple he hadn't seen before they seemed to know each other. Malcolm saw Darian coming over. He smiled , Marcus and Raymond noticed and looked round at who it was . Well they both thought he definitely got it good with the Italian he was gorgeous and especially with that suit to his piercing blue eyes . Darian slid his arm round Malcolms waist and he looked up at Darian smiling at him .

" Darian this is Marcus and Raymond, friends from school " " Hello pleased to meet you " They shook hands Darian looked at Malcolm and back at the boys " Marcus and Raymond got Married " .

" Congratulations to you both " Thanks " Darian looks at Malcolm what's up with him he thought " Enjoy your champagne excuse me " Darian leaves to go up to the VIP area Malcolm looks round at the boys watching him go " Why is he so intense " Raymond asks I feel like I'm blushing he thought looking round at Marcus who was also starring . Malcolm giggles shaking his head " he has that effect on everyone yea he can be intense that's just the way he is " .Malcolm thought and he had thought of that when he first met Darian those years ago .

" I CAN SEE WHY YOU fell l for him " Raymond says looking at Marcus taking his hand " We have went legit haven't we Babe " Marcus nods that's surprising to Malcolm thought good for them " your surprised " Malcolm looks at Marcus then he looks over at Sam who is busy with customers " I am good on you guys " .

" Yeah we decided to leave all that bullshit behind, we love each other too much right babe " Marcus nods again holding Raymond's knee leaning into each other " we want to do our own business now also the blood bank was getting too much too " .

" so we decided to do our own business right babe " Raymond said leaning into his husband Marcus nodded " That's good guys what kind of business you gonna do "

" Not sure yet some ideas were thought about " .

NEIL LOOKED UP AT THE drop in centre again before he went in. They would be closing soon if he didn't hurry to get inside his phone . He checked who it was then disconnected the call Mary once the centre worker came outside and saw Neil hovering. He was looking at his phone . " Neil " He looked up at Mary at the door. He came up the steps. " We were about to close, are you ok" " yes I " .

" C'mon let's get you sorted, we have just made a big pot of Stovies and Tea " great Neil thought just what he needed Ray one the other centre workers came over to Neil handing him his key for his room Neil looking down at the key .

Neil opened the door to his room. It wasn't much but it will do for now just a bed and a shower for the night he thought he stripped and went into the shower with red welts on his leg from the client he had earlier. Some of them liked a bit kink . His but hurt a little so maybe I should stop doing this he thought get myself away somewhere else start new while he washed .

After getting dried fresh clothes Neil went to the canteen a few people there Mary with Ray dishing out the meals Mary looked up at Neil coming over she smiled he looked better with a wash . Mary handed Neil his stovies he got his tea and went over to the table on his own .

" Neil I thought it was you " he looked up someone he knew from the streets she picked up her dog sat her beside her feeding the dog some bits from her plate she looked at Neil he looked Pale she thought and wondered if he was doing ok " Neil you ok " Neil looked up and shook his head Brenda lay her hand on his and squeezed it " it'll get better " " I hope so "

HE SURE HOPED SO NEIL thought about getting sick of trying to make money and wants to do a college course someday something like Centrepoint does but Neil thought he has to get himself clean and sober first .

DARIAN WAS WATCHING the cctv in his office the door chapped Malcolm appeared Darian looked round at him " Hey you " uh oh he's doing it again with the cctv Malcolm came over to Darian " What are you doing "

" Nothing just checking, " Malcolm snorted. That's what security is for he thought Malcolm wrapped his arms round Darians shoulders " You were checking out Raymond and Marcus weren't you " Darian grunted Malcolm smirked reaching up to kiss him looking over at the CCTV .

" You have nothing to worry about there, good guys, they won't cause trouble " " Are you sure? " Malcolm sighed. Why does Durian have to be like this whenever someone new comes into the club?

Malcolm went to move Darian stopped him he looked round at Darian " What is it stud " Darian wiggled his eyebrows Malcolm went over to the door locking it while Darian stood hands in pockets Malcolm leaned against the door smiling cocking his head smirking at Daian .

Darian cocked his head waiting for Malcolm to come to him Darian leaned against the table Malcolm took his hand kissing it sucking Darians fingers his cock twitched Malcolm looked up at him grinning. Darian bent to kiss him Malcolm moved eh what's he playing at Darian thought he went to grab Malcolm . Malcolm grabbed Darian pushing him against the table Malcolm kissed Darians neck going to unbuckle his belt .

Darian took his hand away they looked at each other Darian went to move turning round Malcolm against the table this time licking his ear Malcolm moaned Darians hardness against him " Do you feel that " Darian whispered " mmm " Darian lifted up Malcolm's shirt kissing licking down his back Malcolm whimpered he went to turn Darian lifted him onto the table they kissed chasing each other's tongues .

Malcolm slid his hand down felling Darians cock he hissed Malcolm unzipping his jeans sliding his hand inside Darian doing the same while kissing Malcolm's neck .Malcolm whimpered Darian kissing his neck his ear Malcolm painted closing his eyes while Darian stroked Malcolm .

Sam brought down a Darian tray of coffee he was about to knock on the door when he heard noises from the office. Jesus he thought not again can't they keep their hands off each other Sam thought shaking his head he would have to have words with them soon he thought and decided to go back up to the bar and not leave Darians coffee at the office . "Didn't he want it? " Julia asked when Sam poured the coffee down the sink . " Not exactly he was busy " Julia knew what Sam meant by busy whenever the door was locked that meant not to be disturbed Sam looked pissed off Julia thought I would be to she thought to .

Marcus lay his head on Raymond's shoulder . He lay his arm around his shoulder. " Take me home husband " Marcus sniggered. They kissed, noticed by Sam Marcus and Raymond got up and were about to go when Darian and Malcolm appeared arms round each other all giggly and noticed that Marcus and Raymond were leaving.

" Are you guys going " " Yea it was good to see you Malcolm " Raymond said the three them hugged Malcolm and Darian looked at each other " Darian it was good meeting you " " likewise " they shook hands Malcolm was pleased about that he noticed Sam looking very pissed of working at the bar and wondered what's up with him he will talk to him soon about it probably to do with Geraint .

" I have a feeling we will be back right babe " Raymond leaned into Marcus looking at each other Raymond laying his arm round Marcus " If you want to be a member there's a process to go through and the yearly subscription " .Darian announced looking between Marcus and Raymond .

" Right mates rates " Marcus asked Malcolm, sniggering Raymond lay his arm round Marcus's arm. They looked at each other " C'mon husband time to go home " Raymond beamed at Marcus "I love this man" he thought .

Marcus And Raymond left very strange boys Darian thought watching them go " Right I'll go get my jacket then we can go " Malcolm left to go back into the office Darian went over to Sam before leaving he looks at Darian `` Are you ok " " Fine " Malcolm stared at Sam god he's very tetchy Malcolm thought . " Sam, " Malcolm asked again. Sam looked at him. " I'm fine . " Sam smiled. Malcolm lay his arm on his shoulder, squeezing it, then they hugged . " Talk soon ok " Malcolm whispered Sam nodded " yep " . Sam sighed and thought I shouldn't be angry at him Sam thought but it's just hard right now with Geraint's Cancer and his college work being behind with that . Hopefully soon things will get back to normal .

Cameron was checking on Philip when he heard the car of Darian and Malcolm's arrival home it was just after eleven the club would be shutting in an hour leaving Claudia , Julia to clean lock up with the others Philip had his last bottle and settled down for the night Malcolm peeked in gave Cameron a kiss and disappears into the bedroom for a shower . Darian went into the fridge bringing out orange juice pouring some in a glass Cameron appeared in his pjs Darian looked round at him " How was your dad " " Good he thought Philip was adorable " Well he is adorable Darian thought he has good Genes from his parents .

CAMERON LEANED AGAINST the counter " He has a couple work things when he's here and we thought about making dinner plans " " ok good and how are the chapters coming along " Darian took a drink of his orange juice listening to Cameron leaning on the kitchen table .

Cameron moved nearer to Darian they kissed " Managed to do two more chapters " They heard Malcolm moving out the shower " By the way Sam saw us the other night " Wow Cameron thought maybe they should be more discreet next time . " Malcolm said he looked pissed off about it " .

" understandable I'm gonna go to bed you coming " " I'll be up soon "

They kissed again Cameron left to go upstairs Darian had another glass of juice looking out the window off the conservatory he brought out his phone bringing up Sams not sending out a quick text to him .

Darian " we are here if you need to talk we all love you and care about you and Geraint i know it's frustrating right now but Geraint will get through it "

Sam stopped at the front door to check his text. He opened it up with a text from Darian. Sam smiled thinking of his mood. Tonight he opened the front door just as Geraint was coming out of the kitchen. Sam looked up at him thinking he should be in bed. He went over to him, flung his arms round Geraint's shoulders and kissed .

" Hi " " Hi " Sam hugged Geraint what's up with him he thought kissing his head " Babe you ok " Sam looked at Geraint and nodded " Fine i love you " " Love you to " .

Sam went into the kitchen Geraint following him Sam went into the fridge bringing out a can of bru .Taking a sip " Busy tonight " Geraint asked at the kitchen door .

" not too bad i'll be up in a minute " Geraint touched Sam's face then kissed him then Geraint went up to bed Sam sat at the kitchen table looking at Darians text and wondered why he was feeling pissed off that he caught them the other night .Maybe it's to do with Geraint's Chemo and sometimes he's too tired and takes it out on him there sex life isn't to great right now because if that and maybe feeling frustrated. He texted Darian back saying thanks and he knows .

Sam got into bed he snuggled into Geraint he turned his head to kiss Sam " You're good right "Geraint asked Sam " Yes babe " Geraint moved over to Sam he noticed some hair on the pillow . Shit Geraint thought even though his hair was thinning a bit because of the chemo .

" Geraint " Sam picked up the piece of hair they knew would happen with the chemo and his hair would fall out . " Sam it's ok they said it would happen my hair will grow back ok " . Sam knew that but it still shocked him why Geraint was so calm about it he thought I would be freaking out by now Sam thought if it was me .

" I know I was just shocked, do you want your hat ? " " No, I'm fine. " They both kissed and snuggled into each other. Maybe I shouldn't have been so shocked then about a bit of hair Sam thought but it's part of the chemo which they did say would happen .

Chapter 5

Philip sat on his grandads knee while they ate dinner it suited him Cameron thought and Philip was so good he kept staring at Nathan now that's he's nearly 3 months and getting big Nathan bounced Philip on his knee he giggled " it's a shame Johnny couldn't come to " Cameron asked Nathan and Olivia looked at each other while Darian got up went over to the fridge to bring out more wine .

"Yee it's his exams we didn't want him to miss them since it's his last year of school " ingrid came into the lounge with pudding a chocolate cake Cameron's dads favourite Philip licked his lips noticed by Malcolm he sliced a bit off to give to him Nathan gave him a little bit . " is that nice " . " Uh oh who is gonna like chocolate " . Nathan tickled him Philip giggled .

" How's the writing going Cameron? " Olivia asked, taking a sip of her wine. " Good I'm about to finish Highland Fling 3 and thinking of doing a biography about the three of us. " That's surprising. Nathan thought Cameron took Darians hand and he smiled at him . "We have plans in the future for a new club in Glasgow just looking at plans for now " .Darian announced Nathan was surprised to hear .

" Sounds good we also want to expand the chip shop possibly New Zealand " " that be great dad won't it guys "Cameron said looking between Darian and Malcolm Nathan sniggered nodding "My sister lives there she would take over the site there " Olivia explained to them sounds good the three of them thought .

" MR DARIAN I GO NOW " Ingride comes into the lounge " Thanks Ingrid see you tomorrow " Ingride bows then leaves she seems so sweet Olivia thought Philip yawns time for his nap Malcolm thought he looks sleepy Malcolm gets up going over to Nathan " Can I take him " " Sure " Malcolm looks over at Cameron and Darian nodding . Nathan gets up with Philip `` gotta get the practice in don't i buddy "

Nathan leaves Olivia gets up clearing the plates helping Cameron while Darian goes out to the garden to call Jake see how things are at the club " Does he ever not think about the club " Olivia asks Cameron leaned against the sink while Malcolm fixes the table " Not really but he trusts Claudia , Jake and Julia they have worked for him for a few years .

" Understandable just like your dad with the business can't help but worry " Olivia smiles Cameron nods he knows Darian should not worry about the club but what happened with it when Julius tried to torch it . It was on the back of his mind regarding it which they will never get over .

Nathan comes back downstairs just as Darian was coming back inside " He was out soon as I put him down " " That's our boy " Darian says going over to the table " More wine Nathan " "Please " They go outside to the porch Cameron watched them go sit outside Darian pouring more wine for them .

" Can I say something Darian " Darian looks up at Nathan before he sits down " off course Nathan and I think I know what your going to say " Nathan huffs shaking his head "You are alright I had my doubts but you're alright Darian " Darian giggles nice of him to say Darian thought smiling. " And my grandson he's definitely got your cheekbones " " I certainly hope so Nathan"

" Do i have to worry " Nathan takes a sip of his wine staring at Darian " No Nathan you do not need to worry " .

Darian looks over at Cameron , Malcolm and Olivia in the kitchen clearing up. Malcolm looks over and he smiles at them then carries

on what he is doing in the kitchen "Who wants crackers and cheese?
" Cameron asks from the kitchen door Nathan pats his stomach. He
couldn't eat anymore then Cameron decides to bring it out anyway .

I couldn't eat anymore Malcolm thought coming outside sitting
next to Darian Cameron comes out with Olivia with another bottle of
wine beer . Frank comes out to them going over to Malcolm sitting at
his feet while they chat .

Norman Petrie gushed over Neil while they sat at one of the booths
at the club Neil sipped his beer Norman touched Neil's leg Neil
shivered from.Normans touch " I'm so glad we could do this Neil are
you having fun " " I am Norman " Neil has been meeting up with
Norman for some time now he treated him well which was good thing
Norman is kind to Neil he has never hurt or demanded anything from
Neil " Do you like the jacket Neil " .Neil looked down at his jacket
feeling it and smiling looking at Norman . He did not need to buy it for
him Norman had always bought Neil presents which he did not need
to.

" Yes I do Norman you don't need every time we meet " " Oh but
I want to Neil it makes me happy " Norman touches Neil's face then
kisses his cheek Neil blushed " since we are here we could go to one
the rooms have a little fun " .Norman cocks his head smiling touching
Neil's leg again Norman staring at him .

" Lets just talk first " "Of course Neil do you want anything else "
Neil shook his head Norman took Neils hand while they chatted away
.

Sam comes into the club about to go over to the bar noticing a few
people around and some going through to the rooms when he spots
Norman Petrie with someone Sam looked at again Neil Malcolm did
mention he had seen him a couple weeks ago . Sam thought it was
weird since he looked ok. He thought Sam went to go to the break
room bringing out his phone to call Malcolm .

Malcolm got up going into the kitchen to take Sam's call " Hey what's up " " I just saw Neil at the club with Norman Petrie " wow Malcolm thought sounds like he's ok but weird that he's at the club especially with Norman Petrie . " How did he look " " He looked ok all over each other I'll keep an eye out " .

That would be great if Sam could since he was at home having dinner with his father in law he hoped everything was ok with Neil and Norman Petrie wasn't a bad man he was harmless enough Malcolm thought just as long Norman didn't hurt Neil then Darian would have to interfere .

" THANKS SAM KEEP AN eye out ok catch up soon ok " I will "

SAM WENT BACK OUT WITH Neil still with Norman Petrie he didn't look distressed they seemed to be having a normal conversation which was good Sam thought while he carried on what he was doing at the bar making the drinks cocktails that members requested.

Malcolm came back into the lounge sitting beside Cameron while Darian got the whiskey out looking over at Malcolm wondering who the call was from oh he's on the whiskey now Malcolm thought Darian was looking at him .

" Ok " Cameron asked Malcolm nodded, squeezing Malcolm's hand " Just someone I know came into the club that's all Sam calling me about it "

" Who " Darian asked there he goes all alpha against Neil who is seen at the centre he was with Norman Petrie " Cameron sniggered thinking what he saw with him . " Anyway, I can't interfere .

" I have a friend who works hard for social work. " Olivia said yes that's true Malcolm thought like the college said it's up to the person to ask for help since there are the helplines to call and the centres to go to also for food and shelter .

" I'M GONNA GO TO THE toilet " Neil got up Norman touched his arm he looked down " another drink " " Sure " Sam watched Neil go to the bathroom he excused himself while Jake was sorting out some drinks to go to the bathroom. Is something wrong Jake thought maybe he was just imagining it Jake thought .

Sam washed his hands at the sink Neil came out of the cubicle and saw Sam at the sink he went over to wash his hands " Small world " Sam said Neil looked over at him and nodded " Is Malcolm here " .

Sam leaned against the sink folding his arms `` No he's at home Cameron's dad is visiting " " Oh " Neil dried his hands and looked at Sam . "You ok Neil " Neil snorted and nodded and looked at his watch that looked like a good one Sam thought . " Neil ".

" Go on ask me your wondering where i got all this stuff " " I wasnt are you "

" Escort only when i need the money Norman is good to me Sam it's 9.30 if i dont get back to the centre by 11 well "

Neil went to move Same as Sam " Neil if you need to talk " Neil looked round he wished it was simple to talk he thought " Thanks i better go " .

Finally Norman thought Neil took a long time in the bathroom " Sorry Norman i'm not feeling too great " " Ih not good i could drive you " .

" It's ok I called a taxi " Norman went into his pocket handing Neil money and stuck it in his pocket "Meet soon " . Norman asked Neil to come nearer so they looked at each other .

" I'll call you ok " Neil left he waited outside looking up at the sky shutting his eyes there must be a better life than this he thought . A car horn beeps the arrival of his taxi getting in letting the guy know his destination.

After getting back Neil opened the envelope a thousand he had given him.Neil went under the bed bringing out a box opening it putting the money in the box with the other notes . The door chapped Pat coming in to do checks seeing Neil on the floor ." Ok there Neil " " yes just dropped my phone ". Neil looked up at Pat looking concerned at him. Neil stood up sitting his phone on the bed biting his lip .

" Cutting it fine there " " sorry I bumped into a friend and I was checking out a place for a job to "

Pat came further into the room pleased to hear the news about the possible job "Good where " " I saw on one the notices about a dishwasher just a cafe " Neil hated lying but it was the only thing he could think off he thought " Ok good did you check any off the Out in the board " " Not yet will do tomorrow "

Pat said his goodnight then Neil got changed for bed he was cold shivering a bit he tried not to think about going cold turkey the Coke he got he didn't take threw it away in the toilet he was about to go to sleep when his door chapped Cerys appeared .

" sorry Neil but it's the rules " She held up a cup for him to pee in to test if he had taken anything Neil sighed got up " I did have a couple beers tonight " " Pat said you meet friends " Neil took the cup went into the toilet did his band came back out handing it to Cerys she looked at him thinking he was looking pale " " You ok " " yeah just tired " Cerys do the test with the other care worker Tom it took a few minutes negative good they thought but his drinking tonight they would talk to him about tomorrow.

Tom chapped Neil's door again going inside he was sitting on the bed " Negative " " " Told you I only had a couple beers " Tom came inside he looked pissed off Tom thought " You know it's the rules Neil and we can chat about it in the morning ok " Neil nodded Tom left Neil went back to bed " he thought about the ways he could use the money for get a new flat but the centre would help him with that . Or get away from Scotland, go to London away from the temptation of something to think about in the future or other places to think about .

Chapter 6

Nathan and Cameron sat on the bench in princess street gardens with Philip in his buggy. Cameron and Nathan often visited the park when he was younger and whenever Nathan came home to visit it was their tradition now it was Cameron and Phillips coming to the park weekdays where Cameron would find inspiration for his books .or just to take a breather get out the house and take Frank with them to so he could also get a run about " Are you happy son? " Nathan asked Cameron, looking round at his dad, what a strange thing to say to him. Of course he was happy he had the most amazing husband and now their son. Why would he not think we were not happy?

" YES DAD I'M HAPPY I know you and Darian have difference of opinions and that's fine it's " " Just his nature " Nathan looked round at Cameron smiling and taking a sip his coffee " He grows on you " That he does Cameron thought smiling into himself " Do you remember the first time you came out to me we came here and I knew there was something you were gonna tell me " .Cameron nodded looking at his dad and down at Philip .

" I remember and you said you had an inkling " " And I said I was proud of you and if you needed to talk " Cameron sniggered, yes he remembered, especially his ex moving away and them breaking up . " When you told me about Darian and Malcolm I thought it would cause trouble but seeing you guys progress into s family and my grandson well I can see your a good family "

" Are you sad dad "Cameron asked he just sounded like it Cameron thought " No no I'm happy to be honest the reason Johnny didn't come with us he's having problems " That's not good Cameron thought he thought something was up but didn't want to say anything "He got into the wrong crowd and was taking drugs " " " Shit that's not good dad what about Marina and Jack how are they coping "

" Yea but he's staying with his dad and going to therapy for now we didn't want to say anything till i spoke to you first As for Marina and Jack there rallying round him"

" THAT'S UNDERSTANDABLE dad and it's good that Marina and Jack are there for him to " Philip girdled, spitting out his dummy and grumbling Cameron put his dummy back in " I think he's teething " Nathan looked down at Philip his little cheek red " maybe stop off at the chemist on the way back ".

Good idea Cameron thought we dont want him screaming the place down because he's grumpy right now with his teething and not good with sleeping at night right now because of it then taking turns in the night to check on Philip .

LAUREN SAT ON THE TOILET seat she had done the pregnancy test while Sam and Geraint sat outside waiting on the result Geraint coughed sounding like a right crackle Sam thought " babe " " im fine just a little tickle ".Geraint had a froggy throat for a couple days now Sam thought and he had said to Geraint to speak to the doctor about it next time he goes for his chemo session.

Lauren came out of the bathroom holding the pregnancy test Geraint looked at Sam then looked at Lauren " I'm sorry guys it's negative " They both got up going over to Lauren hugging her looking down at the pregnancy test the negative sign . " It's ok they did say it might not work the first time " Sam said looking at Geraint he nodded. Lauren sat on her couch and she did feel a little disappointed for them . " We'll try again next month, right? " she asked Sam, looking at Geraint he nodded in agreement, smiling at Sam .

" Yes, we'll try next month, " Lauren smiled. She thought " Right for take away. " Sam asked to get out his phone to sort their order out

and to text Malcolm the result " chicken tikka for me.Geraint said "
Sam did the order for the takeaway .While Lauren checked her phone
for her cycle when they could do the next IVF . She joked that they
could use a turkey baster to do it herself . Sam and Geraint thought it
was a silly idea and just did the IVF route again .

MALCOLM CAME OUT OF class checking Sam's text about Lauren
he quickly texted back not to worry maybe the next time then another
text which was from Jenny sunning herself in Spain and had managed
to get a bar job while there good for her he thought she had also meet
up with other backpackers and they were all meeting and moving on
to other countries . Her bar job would last a month and she managed
to get a cheap apartment " Malcolm you coming to the pub ' Kirsten
asked him to look up at Kirsten with a couple other classmates.

" Yea sure that be great " " you don't have to work tonight '

Blair asked while walking along Malcolm texted Cameron and
Darian he was going to the pub with college friends " Not tonight will
go along later after the pub"

IN WETHERSPOONS EVERYONE got there orders and the
conversation flowed Malcolm thought about Sam and Geraint he
would go see them tomorrow " Are you doing another year Malcolm
" Kirsten asked he looked up he was halfway through his second year
and had thought about doing another year or defer for a year " I think
so you " " I did think about leaving it for a year hard going right " .

She was right it was hard going sometimes but he wanted to keep
going with it since he would be doing an internship soon " yea and
especially you with your daughter her age " " she will be turning ten just
wait till Philip turns that age the drama " They both giggled Kirsten

was a lovely person they got on well and shared parenting tips to which helped a lot especially the teething .

" MALCOLM " MALCOLM looked up at Steven with Jordan he got up to hug them and introduced the, to his college friends `` you good "Steven as " yeah you guys love the Tan " Steven looked at Jordan and back at Cameron they had been in the u.s for a holiday and only came back two days ago . " yea I'm good, how was the holiday? "

" Great wasn't it babe " Jordan lay his arm round Steven he nodded " Philip ok " " perfect staring teething " Stevens phone rang he checked the ID Cameron calling him they excused themselves .

" They seem nice " Blair asked " it's Cams best friend his partner " Malcolm explains Blair looking over at them. What is with him? Malcolm thought shaking his head he knew Blair was gay too and got on well with him and the others .

SAM LAID THE HOT WATER bottle into the bed beside Geraint. He wasn't feeling great and decided to go to bed. He had called the 111 with his symptoms and explained that he was getting chemo and had a bit of a cough too and a slight temperature. The woman had told him there was a cold flu bug going around and it would be best he take some paracetamol and go to bed and if his symptoms worsened then to go up to A n E .

" do you need anything else " " No thanks i'm sorry " what's he sorry for Sam though he's not being a bother if that's what he thinks .Sam lay beside Geraint till he fell asleep good Sam thought he needed sleep.

" EXCUSE ME " NEIL had come into a cafe which was called the little coffee shop in The Corner in town after he saw there advert for Help wanted the lady looked round at who was talking she stared at him Neil looked down at himself he looked ok he thought "Yes "

Neil pointed to the sign outside and she looked over " Youre help wanted sign, have you got anyone " " Not yet it's only 16 hours though Tracy can you take over Please " .

The lady who was called Janet took Neil over to the far side to chat to Neil " Have you done this kinda work before " " Yes previously about a year ago " " Will you be able to give references " Damn Neil thought should I be honest with her " I should be able to " Neil bit his Nail Janet stared at him he then sat forward . " To be honest I'm getting my shit together all , I want is to prove to you I'm a good worker any hours will do anything to get out the centre and get my own place " Boy that felt good to let that out Neil thought staring at Janet biting his lip hope she gives me the job Neil thought .

Wow Janet thought she didn't expect Neil to be that honest at least he was " Thank you for your honesty can you fill in the application form everyone needs a second chance right " Janet smiled sliding over application form Neil nodded his phone then went off he excused himself because of his phone disconnected the call he knew who it was from he didn't need to check caller ID .

" I will call you tomorrow arrange when you can start " " I got the job " Neil smiled god he can't believe it he thought she's going to give me a chance " " Yes let's see how you do ok " Neil smiled she seemed ok this Janet woman Neil thought and hopefully 7 can prove i'm a good worker to .

NEIL STOOD OUTSIDE finally something good he thought his phone went to voicemail he checked the message the person cursing on the message to get his ass. Moved or pay the consequences fuck you

Neil thought hiding his rucksack where his money was kept it was still early only 3pm his stomach grumbled Greggs wasn't far and decided to go there keep warm get a pastie and tea .

His phone rang again, ignoring it again, switching it off looking out the window while eating his pastie and drinking his tea now to get my life back, he thought I'm gonna better myself get sober and clean now this time Neil thought .Fuck everyone that gets in my way he thought i should have done it years ago .

DOUG SLAMMED DOWN HIS phone ignoring me again is he the little fucker he thought Bruce one his security came into the office moticing his boss not in a good mood looking round at Thomas he shrugged his shoulders looking over at Doug who was frantically texting Thomas got up going over to Doug taking his phone off him Doug looked up at him thinking why did he take the phone off me when im trying to get in contact with Neil .

" What are you doing " " Love calm down when your mad everybody gets it "

Doug sits back in his chair. Thomas looks over at Bruce who gets the message to leave. Doug was about to say something when Thomas put his finger on his mouth " Not another word ok he will come back I know it " Doug sighed grinning at Thomas who reached over to kiss him . " The Russian " Thomas looked up at Doug while unzipping his jeans " What about him? " Thomas slid his hand inside Doug jeans and began to stroke him. Doug hissed, letting Thomas do his thing while licking his ear . " Don't worry about Russian love, just relax. Ok, let me make you feel good ."

THOMAS SLID DOWN DOUG watched him while he slid of his jeans while Thomas worked his way down taking Dougs cock in his mouth Doug lay his head back going with the feeling Thomas looked up Doug licking his lips holding onto Thomas head he could tell Doug was coming soon jutting out fucking Thomas mouth .

" Shit Thomas I'm " Doug came Thomas took it down his throat he sat up wiping his mouth damn Doug thought Thomas smirking " Beter " "Yes very " Thomas wiped his mouth with a hankie bending over Doug kissing him " Now stop worrying please " Doug nodded getting up fixing himself touching Thomas face they kissed again .

The door chapped one his staff Lola coming in looking pissed off "What is it now " " You speak to Mr Lomax " not again they thought he's gotta stop abusing his staff or he will be bared Doug thought " i'll speak to him Lola " Lola huffed then left she can be fiery that one Doug thought looking at Thomas . " We finish this at home ok " Doug kissed Thomas pinching his bottom Thomas giggled Doug went to the door looked over at Thomas winking at him then left .I so Love that man Thomas thought smirking into himself .

Chapter 7

Neil started his job at the cafe Janet was so nice to him making sure he was ok and everyone else to he wiped his brow and loaded up the dishwasher again Phoebe came round the back for a quick break she seemed nice fiery what is they say about redheads they can be fiery to Shr took some quick breaths counting Neil looked over at her what is she doing he thought . " Sorry, I just needed a breather because the lunch rush was the worst. " Neil smiled, loading more dishes onto the crate. Yes indeed it was a mad rush he thought .

" Neil take a break I'll get Roy make you a burger chips " "Um thanks " Neil loaded the washer and went out front Janet had closed the cafe for an hour so everyone could have a break Neil was enjoying his burger and chips and he thought maybe Roy gave him extra which was kind of him he was beginning to like everyone .

JANET SORTED OUT THE front area she looked over at Neil munching into his food while checking his phone and sighing something must be up she thought he will tell her hopefully " He's a good kid " Roy said Janet looked at him she thought so to " Janet did you " Janet looked at Roy again glaring at him yes she noticed the couple scars on his wrist which he tried to hide earlier.

" I'll talk to him soon ok " Janet touched Roy's arm and nodded looking over at Neil. He's troubled, she thought but she had a good feeling about Neil. He was kinda shy. Sometimes she wanted him to feel relaxed around everyone . In time he will be nervous about starting a new job and getting to know everyone.

" I THINK YOU MAY HAVE Pneumonia Geraint " The Doctor said Geraint looked at Sam how could he have gotten pneumonia was it to do with the cold symptoms he had " Great another thing to ad to my list " he coughed again into his hankie Sam sitting worried " You will have to be admitted we need to keep an eye on you incase of any other infection " Sam and Geraint looked at each other Sam taking Geraint's hand .

" GREAT " GERAINT LOOKED at Sam looking at his phone probably for work to let them know what's happening with Geraint " I'm going to book you in for a scan to and do some more bloods I'll get the nurse come see you "

The doctor left Sam got Geraint's bag to help him into his pjs just as the nurse arrived with an oxygen mask " Hi I'm Claire Doctor has said your breathing's bad Geraint this is to help you it's a steroid "

After the nurse sorted the oxygen Sam's phone rang Malcolm calling he went out to the corridor to take the call " How is he " " pneumonia the docs are giving him oxygen steroids to help his breathing ".

" Not great need anything I can bring it over " " Thanks I'll text you later what we need "

After his call from Malcolm Sam went back inside Lauren also had texted for an update Sam went over to Geraint he kissed his head he could tell he was tired " Malcolm asking how you were and need anything " Geraint nodded Sam sat down beside him taking Geraint hand and kissing it .

" That's kind of him, he's a good friend. " Sam nodded, taking Geraint's hand. He looked so pale, he thought and Sam hoped the antibiotics steroids would help Geraint .Sam hated seeing Geraint like this and unable to help him but he was in the right place Sam thought .

DOUG AND THOMAS SAT up at the VIP area chatting to some Customers one his security Grant came over to him " Boss it's Viktor Rolf " Thomas looked at Doug Viktor wasn't supposed to arrive till tomorrow why is he early they thought Doug got up buttoned his jacket looking down at Thomas he nodded at him .He looks Nervous Thomas thought the man does make everyone fear him .

Lina, their concierge, was coming over with Viktor beside her and his two security men. He was a big man and a very dangerous man to be involved with. Lina gave a faint smile when Doug and Thomas came over to them. Viktor looked very serious. Doug thought he looked at Thomas and looked back at Viktor.

" Viktor this is an unexpected surprise " Doug held out his hand for Viktor to shake which he ignored " Yes I come to have a drink ok " " Yes yes off course please come up to our VIP area anything to drink Viktor"
.

" VODKA YES' ' LINA left to order Viktor his vodka and they went up to the vip area Rauol one the waitress brought over the drinks and the bottle Vodka Viktor asked for while sitting on the table then left .

" How long will you be in Scotland for Viktor? " Thomas asked while Viktor drank two glasses of Vodka. The boy could drink " Youn drink with me, yes. "" Of course Doug poured himself a glass and Viktor clinked glasses. " No drink, " Viktor asked Thomas Doug, looking at Thomas .

" No I'm unable to, I have a condition and have to take medication " Viktor grunted and nodded looking back at Doug " The boy " shit Doug thought how's he gonna explain about Neil going awol " Neil's sick he had tonsillitis " " Ahh to bad he ok " .

" Just needs to rest right babe " Thomas said Doug nodded smiling while Viktor drank " Excuse me " Doug got up what's he doing Thomas thought going through the back and coming back a few minutes later with two off there regulars that Viktor might like .

Doug put his arms round Eli and Ben looked at him and up at Viktor who sat forward Doug nodded at the two of them to go up to sit with Viktor " Put a smile on and make him happy " Eli huffed looking at Ben who both went up to Viktor .

" Viktor this is Eli and Ben " Eli and Ben sat at each side pouring Viktor another vodka. He smiled looking between the two boys while his two security sat at the other side looking around the club. Will they relax? Doug thought it was making him nervous .

That's a relief Doug thought but why isn't Neil checking in what's up with him maybe i should get someone to check in on him wherever he is .He brought out his phone writing a text to Neil Thomas came over to Doug he looked at Thomas . " Babe you need to calm down "

Doug looked at Thomas. He's right. I'm getting uptight over nothing but when Viktor is in town he wants to be treated well at the club Doug took Thomas and they smiled at each other . " Sorry the man drove me crazy " " I Know " .

NEIL STEPPED OUT OF the cafe. He looked round at the others coming out. Janet and Roy lived upstairs " Neil " Neil went over to Janet " The rota check and see if it's ok we give it to everyone " Janet handed Neil the envelope he thanked her for it hopefully more shifts . He was beginning to like the place and the people too .

" We're going to the pub. Neil wants to come. " Phoebe asked. That was kind of them , but he was pretty tired from today and he was quitting drinking from now on " Thanks another time I'm pretty bushed .

Neil got the bus back to the centre which would only take fifteen minutes. Instead of walking he checked his phone messages from Doug and Thomas and one from a potential flat that Jan had messages about he would talk to her about later as for Doug he can stew Neil thought .

As for Doug he didn't reply back let him stew for a bit more same with Thomas waa different from Doug he wasn't as head strong as Doug Neil got off the bus the centre was only just minutes up the road there were a couple beggars he passed and thought back to the time he did that for a couple nights it was long and hard road back then .

Neil rang the bell Brendan one the centre workers answered the door letting Neil in Jan was on shift she smiled at him when he passed he nodded his head going straight to his room he sat on the bed and lay down I should get a shower he thought . The door chapped Brendan appeared " if your hungry were making baked potatoes and cheesy beans " " Ok I'll be along soon' ' Brendan went to go he turned round " Neil " " I know Brendan' ' Jan appeared with the sample pot Brendan left .To help out at the kitchen .

Jan sat on the chair holding the sample pot. Neil looked at her "How has your day been? " Jan asked Neil to scrub his face and thought his good day at the cafe was busy. He didn't even think about using today or touching any alcohol. " Good Jan and Roy are so nice I can't believe how lucky I've been " .

" We are proud of you Neil, you're doing well in the flat. It's available for you whenever you want to view it "" Great when " .

Jan said she would take him to view it and if he wanted it he can move in anytime " Jan I'm really grateful and giving me a good reference to Janet and Roy I'm gonna do it get clean and I wanna keep working at the cafe I really like the people "

" Good now we're having group therapy later, will you come along if you want to? "" I might well do this sample right, " Jan snorted. Neil took the pot, went into the bathroom doing his business and gave it to Jan after .

" if your hungry come have food ok "

AFTER NEIL HAD HIS shower changed he was tired he lay on his bed checking his phone for Any other messages one From Norman Petrie asking when they could meet Neil didn't reply I think I should get a new phone he thought or SIM card . The door chapped Jan came in standing at the door " Negative " great Neil thought then thinking he would use it while working Neil stood up " When is group therapy starting".

" Right now " ok Neil thought today to get my life back and start with group therapy but was it for him.to listen to others tell their story or tell him he can only try it and see if it is for him .

Chapter 8

A few days later Geraint was getting better the steroids was helping he didn't need to use the oxygen much now the doctors thought another few days in the hospital to make sure the pneumonia clears his chemo had to be stopped for now he was looking in the mirror in his room more his hair had come out and his hair was in patches . He stuck his beanie on and his sweatshirt and the nurse came into his room " Geraint you're scheduled for another scan later and Dr Morris will be along later " " Ok Thanks " .

GERAINT TEXTED SAM with an update while he was in class. Good Sam thought that he's feeling better so he would go along to the hospital later and take some supplies so he didn't like the hospital food. Not everyone liked hospital food, he thought but at least he was eating better, which was good, Sam thought .

NEIL SWORE INTO HIMSELF stupid damn coffee machine while trying to make an espresso for practice he did not a bad job with the last one " They should invest in a new one " Phoebe sighed standing watching him yea he thought so to while the machine coughed and sputtered Neil banging on it sighing .

" Excuse me, can I order? " " Just a minute on our machine. " Neil looked up and came across an amazing green-eyed biker jacket holding his helmet and amazing hair. Neil thought " it's ok I don't need a coffee. I'll have this and can I. Order a toastie too " .

" I'll get that " Phoebe took biker guys order while Neil sorted the machine he checked it again doing another coffee which came out fine he was blushing Phoebe thought she sniggered Neil looked at her what's she laughing at " He is cute right " they both looked over at him Neil thought definitely thought he was cute and was having a flush and his cock was doing things since he went celebate for a while just to see if he could be able to .

" Not too bad " " Oh c'mon you have eyes I have eyes " Phoebe playfully punches Neil's arm they both giggled. What is funny is Janet thought coming through from the office it was good to see Neil happy . " What's funny? " Phoebe whispered to Janet. She looked over at the biker guy. Yes, he was cute, she thought and thought he had been in a few times before .

" Neil a word. " Janet asked. Neil looked at Phoebe who shrugged her shoulders. Neil followed Janet into the office. She sat at the desk going into the drawer looking round at Neil . " Your wages Neil since we didn't get your bank details in time " .

" Oh sorry about that, yeah I'll sort that out. " " No hurry , if you prefer cash in hand it's no problem. " Maybe that would be better. Neil thought Janet handed him the envelope, he thanked her and went back out to work. Just as the biker guy was leaving Neil watched him go stuffing his money in his jeans pocket .

Phoebe noticing Neil smiling into himself while she made up an order he is blushing to Phoebe Noticed as well what is up with him. Maybe it has to do with the customer .

GERAINT SAT OUTSIDE Dr Morris clinic and the nurse went to check when he would be taken. Another person waited at the clinic to keep checking his phone while he texted Geraint was also waiting for

Sam to arrive. He was running a bit late because the college running behind Sam had mentioned that their Essays were to be checked .

" These Clinics never on time " Geraint looked round at the guy who had an English accent Essex. Maybe Geraint thought " Yea i know are you waiting on someone ".

" I am and you " " Yes Husband i'm Geraint " Thomas nodded looking along the corridor again and wishing Doug would hurry up what is keeping him Thomas

" Thomas and yes mine to he's also running late " Geraint sniggered then coughed that didn't sound good Thomas thought " sorry little set back i have cancer"

" ahh reason for the beanie " Geraint nodded " you " " Huntingtons had it for two years now .

" Ouch, " Thomas smiled and nodded. He checked his phone again. " How long have you had it? Geraint asked Thomas, looking round at him. " I was diagnosed last year. I get check ups every few months. Just recently my symptoms flared up again, which is a pain ."

" Not great, ahh , finally my other half " Sam came walking up the corridor. Thomas looked round at who Geraint was talking about, a nice looking grungy type just like Geraint tall . " Sorry traffic and college " Sam bent to kiss Geraint and noticed the guy on the other side . " ok " " yea there running late this is Thomas " Sam looked round Thomas looked up and smiled " Hello is this one been chewing your ear off " Sam pointing his finger at Geraint .

Sam looks round at Geraint Thomas sniggers "Not at all we have been comparing notes " Thomas hears the door opening looked round just as Doug appears thankfully he thought . " That's my Dougie " Sam and Geraint look round at who Thomas is talking about . Flash suite business type Sam grinned reminding him of Darian with his suites .

" Geraint " Geraint looks round at Dr Morris they both stand up Geraint looks round at Thomas `` Good to meet you " " you to " Sam and Geraint disappear into Dr Morris office .

" Sorry I'm late " Thomas looks up at Doug smiling at him " it's ok there running behind at least you're here now " Doug bends to give Thomas a kiss on the cheek they bumped heads Doug touching Thomas face .

Thomas sits down Doug beside him he takes Thomas and they look at each other " Dougie it's just routine ok " Doug nods he hates hospitals and wishes there was something a cure for his husband for his Huntington's disease . "Do you need anything " " I'm fine just you " . Thomas lays his head on Doug's shoulder .

Doug pats his head he hated these hospital visits but they were necessary since Thomss condition was getting worse now for the past few months now .

NEIL CAME OUT OF THE mobile shop after his purchase of a new mobile new no he will keep the other one just in case anyone needed him on the old no he stuffed his purchase in his rucksack he would sort the new phone when he gets back to the centre later first he had to go somewhere first he would get flowers first to take with him .

At the cemetery Neil bent down in front of his fathers grave leaving the flowers. It would have been his birthday today. Neil stood up wiping the tears from his eyes. He couldn't believe it's now seven years since he passed and since then his mum has remarried . He hasn't seen his mum and siblings for some time now, not that he would be welcome by his step father since they didn't get on most of the time . " Happy birthday Dad " Neil stood up and looked up at the sky fighting back the tears. Get yourself together, Neil thought .

NEIL WAS ABOUT TO LEAVE the cemetery and go back to the centre he passed a couple people and keeping his head down not recognising who it was while walking along " Neil " Neil froze he recognised the person's voice he looked round his sister Meg with someone she smiled and took her arm away from the guy coming over to Neil .Shit it's been a while since he saw Meg Neil looked at the guy she was with and looked at Meg again .

" It is you " "Hey Meg " Meg came over hugging her brother he felt thin she looked at him and looked back at the guy " This is Brian " They nodded at each other " Neil where have you been it's been a while " .Neil stuffed his hands into his pockets looking at Meg chewing his lip should I tell her the truth or sugar coat it he thought .

" Around Meg I " " Can you wait let's get a coffee there's so much to tell you please " " um .. ok " . No harm in having a coffee with his sister. Neil thought they should catch up, he guessed .

AFTER MEG VISITED HER dad the three of them went to costas for a coffee Meg told him about Brian how long they have been together and how they met and were moving in together soon. It was great to hear Neil thought Brian seemed nice he could tell . Meg went to the toilet Brian went to pay which he didn't need to and came back to sit with Neil "She talks about you a lot " " She does " that's surprising Neil thought but good to hear that Meg talked about him .He smiled thinking that gave him a boost they should maybe try keep in touch better to .

" You don't have to worry about Meg Neil, I love her and we plan to get married " . That's great to hear Neil thought great news for once Meg came back they went outside Meg wanted to keep in touch they exchanged no's but Neil asked Meg not to tell their mum about them meeting yet which Meg promised not to until Neil was ready .To see his mum again in the future they said their goodbyes and Meg promised she would catch up with Neil soon .

" HOW DID YOU THINK he looked " Meg asked Brian when they got in the car he did look like he wasn't using she hoped "He looked ok why " " I just hope he's getting clean Brian " Brian touched Megs knee she looked over at him smiling hopefully they will meet soon talk about things then . Should she mention it to her mum maybe not until they meet up again she would talk to Nei

About that the next time .Her mum had thought about Neil a lot to Meg .

TEARS RAN DOWN NEIL'S face watching the house seeing his sister shook him a bit he had thought many times to contact his family and today brought it all back going to visit his dads grave Neil hid behind the tree while he watched the house so he couldn't be seen he huddled into himself while he watched the house . This is silly Neil thought but all he wanted was to see his Mum and give her a big cuddle

.

" TAKING THE BUCKET out " Neil's mum Lynsey shouted, coming out the house going over to the bucket taking it to the edge the pavement she huddled into herself gosh it's cold she thought . " Mum can't I play with my iPad game " Neil's brother Patrick asked from the door " Only for half an hour " Neil smiled that his little brother had grown so fast he thought he was 14 now and wondered if he was doing ok and not getting into trouble . He was getting taller from the last time he had seen his little brother and wondered how he was doing .

Lynsey hoovered looking out to the houses and a gut feeling came over her " Lynsey what are you doing it's freezing " Lynsey looked over at her husband John standing at the door she looked round again maybe it was my imagination she thought and went back inside . " Are you ok " " Yea fine " John looked out before he shut the door what's up with her he thought she saw something .Lynsey went into the kitchen switching on the kettle John came into the kitchen behind her . " Lynsey what's up " John asked hoovering at the door Patrick came into the kitchen going int9 the fridge for a can of coke and left .

" It's nothing, I'm fine cuppa " " Yes please " .

Neil leaned against the wall wiping his tears. That was really stupid he thought someday he would pluck up the courage to go to the front door next time but would be welcomed back into the family. That's what he would need to find out , so he left to go get the bus back to the centre. I have to get clean and sober, that's the main thing Neil thought then Mum would see how I was whenever I get clean and sober that was the main objective Neil thought .

NEIL LIFTED UP HIS jeans taking off his sock, the bracelet on his ankle he thought for a minute I'm not gonna be shackled to anyone anymore he thought and decided to take it off Neil held it up that feels good he thought now onto the next step of getting my life back . Flinging the bracelet in the bucket he then went to get out a drink from his bag and looked at the rubbish bin tutting to himself going back over to the bin bringing out the bracelet and stuffing it in his back. Keep it in there for now for safe keeping .

Chapter 9

The door chapped on Dougs office door he looked up just as Neil appeared. Finally he thought after 3 weeks of not contacting him Doug shut his laptop, Neil coming nearer to the desk he looked ok Doug thought what had he been up to this past three weeks . Has he been ok or been on a bender he didn't look like he had Doug thought

" Finally decided to show your face then " Neil sighed sitting on the chair beside the table " Doug " " Dont Doug me don't you realise we were worried " Neil snorted Doug glared at him what's funny he thought glaring at Neil .Aren't I allowed to be worried Doug thought glaring at Neil he did look better which was good he thought.

" When have you ever been worried about Doug? I'm here . I'm getting clean. " Wow Doug thought it was good for him. " Good for you. " Neil went into his pocket, bringing out the bracelet looking down at it, then putting it on the table .Doug looked up at Neil, surprised at what he had done, why now what he's got planned for the future wh.

" Neil, have you thought about this " " I have been doing my own thing now Doug. I'm getting sober and getting Clean. Doug's phone beeped text from a couple of clients who had arrived . " I don't need the money anymore. I got a job I like and the people I work for are really nice to me".

Doug looked up the door and chapped Thomas coming inside and was shocked to see Neil come over to him hugging him " Neil you came back " ." No Thomas i'm not back " looking over at Doug Thomas stood up going over to Doug leaning against his chair Doug looked up at him then over at Neil .

" What's going on " Thomas asked " Neils quitting " what the hell Thomas thought Neil got up Doug went into his drawer bringing out his cheque book why he was quitting Thomas thought .

" Neil Mr Irving is here you know he pays well how about keeping him sweet tonight " Neil sighed looking between Doug and Thomas he didn't plan to stay and just leave but Mr Irving did pay well one last time wouldn't hurt he thought but he wasn't going to do anything else with him tonight though just chat with him keep him sweet he guessed .

GINA WAS SERVING LENOARD Irving his whiskey up at the Vip area she left him some nibbles so Neil went round to the bar picking up the champagne he took two glasses Gina smiled hugging him pleased to see Neil .And he looked well to she thought and was pleased to see that . He was quitting in no way Gina thought .

Lenoard smiled when he saw Neil come over to him with the champagne sitting beside him " Neil lovely to see you " " Mr Irving you to champagne " Neil held up the champagne bottle Mr Irving patted the chair beside him . Cocking his head glad to see Neil .

Neil poured him a glass for him and Neil clinked their glasses and took a sip. Thomas appeared checking on everything was ok and went up to the vip area. Neil and Mr Irving were chatting. He thought he was sweet . " Everything is fine now that Neil is here " Leonard touched Neil's leg he smiled looking over at Thomas " Anything else you need Mr Irving let us know " Leonard nodded Thomas left to go back into the office letting Doug know all was ok with Neil and Mr Irving .

" HOW HAVE YOU BEEN Neil " Mr Irving touched Neil's Leg again he crunched smiling at Mr Irving " Good just busy with work what about you " .

Mr Irving took a sip of his Champagne and looked at Neil ` ` Same but not too busy " Neil nodded listening to Mr Irving's plans for his trailer truck business .

All Neil could think about was getting out of here soon. I'm over this now, he thought not doing this shit anymore .

PHILIP SQUEALED, SPLASHING in the water at the local pool Malcolm had him on his knee in the kids area. He certainly liked being in the poolHe thought Cameron was sitting beside him laughing at Philip with his bathing suit and arm bands on Darian and Nathan over at the other side watching them . They had taken some photos and videos of them in the pool and it was great to see Philip enjoying himself in the pool Nathan was pleased to know .

" WELL WE WILL DEFINITELY have to bring him back, " Cameron said. Taking Philip sitting him on his lap, he kicked out his legs squealing again. " I think so " A couple of other parents with their kids also sat over at the side enjoying the pool. It wasn't too busy , which was good Cameron and Malcolm thought. While they dipped Philip's feet in the water he squealed again. Cameron and Malcolm laughed at his actions .

" HE SURE LIKES THE water doesn't he? " Darian looked at Nathan and back at his son. Yes he did he and Cameron , Malcolm had talked about bringing him to the pool to see if he would like it which he did thankfully. " He does " Darian took some pictures of Philip again splashing about in the water and a couple videos to which he will send to Aida . " Darian I was wondering if I could look after Philip let you guys have a night out. What do you think? " Good idea Darian thought it's been a while since they had a proper night out since Philip's arrival even though they had a couple nights at the cinema .

" That will be great Nathan I'll let Cameron and Malcolm know " Darians phone beeped of a text he fished his phone out his pocket Nathan watched on while Darian checked a text from Jake and Claudia all ok at the club Darian would go along later . Nathan noticing Darian texting whoever it was back it must be stressful owning a club Nathan knows that with his business with the chippy .

" work doesn't stop right " Darian looks at Nathan that's true he thought putting his phone back in his pocket " True like yourself Nathan " Cameron came over to them with Philip Darian got up going over to them kissed Philips head " gonna get changed he's enjoyed it haven't you buddy " .Cameron kissing Philips head bouncing him I think he is tired out now Darian thought while Cameron went off to get changed .

MALCOLM AND CAMERON went off to get changed with Philip Darian and Nathan would wait in the cafe area for them. Darian got them both coffees while they waited " Nathan you don't have to worry about us we're doing good " Nathan knew that when Cameron told him when they went to the park with Philip . " I know sometimes I do though but I can see that you guys are happy and now my grandson is here I do hope you guys will visit in the summer " . That was the plan Darian thought of going to visit Nathan and also plan to visit family in Italy too .

" We will , we talked about it and were thinking of going to Italy to visit family too " " That's good I've always liked Italy. The views are amazing. You have family in Altamore right? " Darian had cousins and an uncle that owned a restaurant there and he wanted to take Malcolm and Cameron there . They had only been to Sorrento and had planned to visit more places in Italy .

LATER THAT NIGHT WHILE at the club Cameron sorting out a tray of Champagne to take up to the vip area Malcolm sorting out a tray of drinks and nibbles to take to one of the rooms and Darian in the office sorting out this month's payments with Claudia .who was to pay there monthly subscriptions and who was late with payments he had emails to go over also while at the club .

NEIL CAME INTO THE club his rucksacks over his shoulder and huddled into one his jacket zipped up and his beanie hat on he looked round the room he didn't see Malcolm was here tonight he wondered he wiped his eyes going over to the bar . " Excuse me is Malcolm here " Jake looked around at who was asking and he looked upset at the guy he thought.`` He is are you ok " Neil shook his head Jake came round and took Neil over to one the booths he was upset and was about to cry Shit Jake thought what has happened that he has got upset about . Jake got out his phone sending a text to Malcolm. He looks up at Neil looking a little calmer now .

Malcolm came round to the bar to Jake who pointed to Neil over at the booths he told him he looked upset. Why did Neil come here, he thought and not go to the centre? He can't do this to Malcolm whenever there is help needed he couldn't get involved .

" Neil what's wrong " Malcom sat on the other side giving Neil a drink of water " Neil took the glass and drank some of the water he looks up at Malcolm I'm sorry I know it's against the rules but it's the only place I could think of " Neil wiped his nose rubbing his eyes what is he gonna do now he thought .

" Neil are you high " Neil shook his head the coke had worn off a while ago " I fucked up Malcolm the centre they told me " Malcolm looked round at Cameron watching him from the bar he can't get involved he thought but what can he do he can't just tell him to go and not care .Malcolm looks back at Neil he just looks so lost right now Malcolm thought .

" Neil I'm sorry you know I can't talk to you about this " " I know I'm sorry I really am but your the only person that understands " That's true Malcolm thought and I got my shit together and if it wasn't for Sam and him deciding that god knows what there life would be like now if Darian wasn't around .

The door chapped at the office Malcolm came inside with Neil Darian and Claudia looked at each other while Malcolm helped with Neil Cameron coming into the office after them " Check in this later Claudia " Darian said Claudia left Cameron made Neil a coffee and gave it to him he thanked Cameron so thoughtful off him Neil thought . Malcolm got up, getting out his phone, excusing himself to call .

" I'm sorry Mr Longstrome I tried " Cameron looked up at Darian leaning against the table he was listening to Neil rant how he fucked up if he hadn't went to Eden club temptation was in the way Malcolm came back into the office . Neil looked up at Malcolm coming back into the office . " I called Marcus and Raymond and they will be here soon " .

" Why them? " Neil asked Malcolm as Neil Cameron got up and went over to Darian. He laid his arm round Cameron's shoulder. " Neil you can talk to them Marcus and Raymond have gone legit now you can trust them like I said to you before I can't be involved " Neil snorted. yea he will believe it when he sees them he thought .And he knows Malcolm can't get involved in his business but he was grateful that he called Marcus and Raymond so he can chat to them .

" ive also spoke to Jan she wasnt working there a couple new staff Neil she said you kicked off " fuck he thought he remembered now when they said he had to leave because of his behaviour . " Yea maybe i shouldn't have done that " Neil did feel bad about that but he got angry at himself that he was rude to the staff at the centre .

The door-chapped opening Marcus and Raymond appeared. Neil looked over at them. Malcolm took them outside to talk to them first . " He's in a bad way guys, could you talk to him?" " Of course we can " .Marcus and Raymond looked at each other . "It's because of course I can't get involved " Marcus patted Malcolm's shoulder and nodded. " We understand " Marcus looks at Raymond, their silent understanding .

They went back inside Darian , Cameron and Malcolm left them to talk and went out to the bar Marcus and Raymond would let them know when they finished the three of them sat at the bar . "Jake " " Yes boss " Jake came over to them he looked over at who Darian was looking at .

Darian looked round at Mr Bailey he looked back at Jake jk" Can you remind Mr Bailey about his bill please" " Sure boss " Oh Jake thought he's late with his payment again maybe .And Darian doesn't like that he's a good boss that way Jake thought .

JAKE WENT OVER TO MR Bailey with his drinks and sat his bill beside him " What is this " " Your Bill Mr Bailey Darians asked if you could' ' Mr Bailey looked over at Darian chatting to Malcolm and Cameron . " it must've slipped my mind ill sort that " . Mr Bailey taking a sip of his drink shaking his head . He is certainly on the ball about memberships, how embarrassing he thought .

" Mr Bailey Darians asked if you could pay now " Mr Bailey looked round at his friend, very embarrassed he thought he excused himself to go and sort out his membership bill Jesus the man needs to take a chill pill he thought .i would have got round to it Mr Bailey thought .

MARCUS AND RAYMOND came out to the bar explaining what Neil had told them he also had been working at Eden club which Darian had not heard about Marcus and Raymond had . Neil also agreed he would stay with Marcus and Raymond till he finds a new place Malcolm thought it was kind of them to do so just as long he didn't fuck it up and help out Marcus and Raymond .With the house chores and rent if he could Malcolm thought .

Darian fired up his laptop looking for Eden club Neil sat on the couch he had calmed down now which was good Darian thought Cameron and Malcolm behind him to look over this Eden club see what the fuss is about it Darian looked round at Cameron and Malcolm while checking through this Eden club similar to Darians club he thought .

" What are you doing " Malcolm asked while Darian checked out membership and guest prices he looked between Cameron and Malcolm smirking is he doing what I think he's doing Malcolm thought " Research right love " Cameron smiled shaking his head " Darian you know I can't " Malcolm said Darian looks up at him again . " Not to worry Cameron and I will go for research purposes right love " raising his eyebrows smirking Cameron shook his head he better not kick off or trample all over the place Cameron thought .

Darian clicked on guest and how many would be with him which would be Cam'ron oh Darian thought non members have a fee to pay my non members don't need to well that's a no no from him he thought " What to say are we available " Darian asks looking at Cameron `` " Any day " " Friday then " Cameron sniggers he comes round to Darians side looks at the computer then at Darian . " How much for a guest " looking at Darian " I can afford it " Darian smirks seriously, this man is going to give me a heart attack one day .

" THANKS FOR THIS GUYS I really appreciate it " Neil says walking into Marcus and Raymond's home they look at each other and back at Neil " Anything to help you can stay as long as you want right babe " Marcus looks at Raymond who nods " besides we have a spare room for now "

" For now " what do they mean for now and how can they afford this place? He thought " Your room is just here " . They walk along the hallway coming to the spare room Raymond switches on the light revealing the spare room a couple boxes on the floor single bed . " I'll get you towels " Neil sits down in his rucksack looking round the room . " Neil it'll get better I promise " Neil looks round at Marcus he hopes so I want to get sober and clean . Raymond comes back with the towels and sits them on the bed .

" Can I get a shower " " Course you can anytime you want we will leave you to it " There about to leave Marcus looks round at Neil " Neil this is a drug free home we don't do that anymore " " Babe let's not right now ok " Marcus nods at Raymond he's right they can talk about things soon but or now let him rest .

NEIL SINKS INTO THE bath that feels good. He thought his phone beeped and he would check it soon while enjoying the bath. I can do this. He thought it was just a glitch. I want to better myself, definitely get clean and sober and work at the coffee shop. He also thought about college courses he could do something like Malcolm is doing .

MARCUS AND RAYMOND sat on the couch, Marcus arm round Raymond shoulder watching tv and drinking tea. When Neil came into the lounge they looked up at him. He looked so much fresher now that he had the bath . " Better " " So good guys I'm gonna crash I'm wiped out " .

" UNDERSTANDABLE SEE you in the morning " Neil nodded and went into his room getting under the covers so good he thought he was dog tired, his mind playing over things he tried not to think about until he eventually fell asleep .

A day later Neil walked into the cafe Phoebe looked round he's finally come back she thought she smiled at Neil he nodded Janet came out from the back good he's ok she thought they went into the office Janet sat down looking at Neil " you wasn't sick were you " Neil looked down shaking his head Janet had an inkling something was up with Neil when he didn't come to work those couple days .

" i fucked up Janet I understand if you sack me but I " " Neil your not getting sacked " Neil thought is she serious he thought I'm not getting the sack " For real " Janet stood up went over to Neil and hugged him this is weird Neil thought she must like me not to sack him .Tears singing his eyes it was a lot for people to care for him and making sure he was ok .Neil wrapped his arms round Janet tears running down his cheeks .

" NEIL THE MINUTE YOU walked into the cafe I knew there was something about you " Janet wiped her eyes same with Neil " I got kicked out the centre "

Janet looked round at Neil he doesn't have to tell her she thought Neil sat on the chair Janet sat beside him " I'm staying with friends till I get a place they didn't need to but my friend Malcolm fixed it for me " " that's good " The door chapped Roy appeared he looked between Janet and Neil . " Are we good? " Neil nodded. He got up. " I better get to work. " Neil left, leaving Janet and Roy .

" what happened " " he's had a rough time Roy and I think we can help him with something "

JANET STOOD WATCHING Neil walk round the flat upstairs from the cafe that they own Janet and Roy live across the landing from it to Are they serious they want to give Neil the Fiat even though they use it for storage sometimes Neil looked round at Janet " Janet are you sure " " yes Roy and I talked about it £50 pound a month I'm being generous about that " .Janet looked at Roy he nodes looking back at Neil .

" of course that's fine Janet thank you " " as long as you don't fuck it up stay clean go to meetings " Neil smiled won't fuck it up he thought and he was planning on still going to meetings " Janet whose flat was it " Janet looked at Roy he nodded Neil looked bettern them chewing his lip .

Janet bit her lip was about to go out she looked round at Neil " Our son Jamie he died two years ago " " Oh I'm sorry to hear that ."

" THANKS NEIL JUST KEEP out of trouble ok that's all we ask " Roy said just before he left that's what I plan to do Neil thought and he was thankful for Their generosity .Looking around the flat Neil smiled and nodded that things are progressing.

Chapter 10

Darian and Cameron drove to Eden club which was outside of Edinburgh twenty minutes drive they both wondered why not in the city like Darians they came to a gated place ok why gated Darian thought he looked at Cameron who shrugged his shoulders . Darian rolled down the window pressing the buzzer on. Within a second the person spoke asking for the code he was given Darian gave them the code then the gates opened codes Darian thought its all very mysterious he thought should I do that to he thought Cameron looking at him he is thinking about stuff Cameron thought .

Darian stopped the car at the parking Cameron touched his arm Darian looked at him "Don't worry I'll be on my best behaviour " Darian smirked Cameron huffed shaking his head knowing very well he won't he thought they got out the car looking up at the building looked at each other "Do you think I should have the other place like this " Cameron looks at Darian shaking his head " What " " Nothing c'mon " . Cameron laying his arm round Darians he grins at Cameron while they walk up the steps .

Cameron presses the bell then it is opened by a woman in a very tight gold dress and hair pulled back with the biggest smile on her face " Welcome to Eden " " Thank you " Darian looks at Cameron and at the lady " I'm Inga please come in Mr Longstrome, Mr Fraser " .

They go inside and they look around Darian nods huh he thought decor could be better " Please come through a Champagne for you both " A waiter arrives in a ridiculous bow tie black waistcoat and black trousers they both take the champagne and follow Inga to their table . They look around purple decor ghastly colour Darian thought Cameron knew what he was thinking and glared at him dunking his side Darian looks at Cameron wondering why he did that they looked around and noticed a few things . The bar over at the side and multiple tables scattered around booths Vip was up on another level they noticed . Cameron thought it didn't look too bad different from Darians club, maybe some similar bits but not too much .

Inga came into the office leaned against the door Doug and Thomas looked up at her they looked at each other " God he's intense " Doug shook his head looks at Thomas " keep him sweet Inga " Do I have to aren't you coming to introduce yourself " Inga sighed she didn't want to deal with Darian on her own .And slip up if he asks anything because she didn't want to be the bad one and get on Doug's bad side .

' I will " Inga tutted then left she's mad he thought Doug looked up at Thomas then Doug stood up buttoned his jacket " Right let's see what the competition looks like " Thomas hugged Doug kissed his cheek " Please be nice babe "" off course " . Thomas wrapped his arms around Dog's waist. They kissed. Thomas went to move Doug grabbing his arm and he looked up at Doug . " We could go home early, " Doug said, smiling , cocking his head .

Thomas came nearer to Doug sliding his hand down cupping Dougs cock he hissed " Maybe if you're a good boy " Doug shook his head Thomas taking his hand " c'mon you " leading him out the door .giggling at each other I will get him back for that Doug thought .

Not to bad Champagne Darian thought when the bottle had been brought over compliments by the owner nice Darian thought " Are you enjoying your Champagne love " " I am " he will only have the one since he is driving Eden club was getting busy now they both noticed and some members were disappearing round the back where the rooms were . Darian looked at Cameron and they kissed " while we were here " Cameron smiled, touching Darians face. That's maybe what Cameron

thought .Besides they were only here to check it out Cameron thought
.

" Mr Longstrome, Mr Fraser " They both looked around at who spoke to them two men standing smiling at them the one who spoke very tall brown hair and well dressed Darian noticed " Doug Martin " Doug held out his hand for them to shake " My partner Thomas " " pleased to meet you both' ' Darian said looking between Doug and Thomas .Very polite Darian thought and they seemed kinda nervous to maybe it was because of their arrival maybe .

" Likewise " " I do hope everything is to your liking " Doug asked looking between them and Thomas" Your staff are very polite haven't they Cameron " Cameron nods yes they have Cameron thought hopefully they are like that all the time

" Yes they have " Doug looks at Thomas nodding at him " Mr Fraser I expect you're doing research for your next book Cameron smiles an avid reader he expects " Thomas asked " Yes I am doing some research for my next one thanks and busy writing and I have a plan for another " Cameron looks at Darian who winks at him .

" GREAT, I HAVE READ that the highland fling loved it. Thomas beams looking at Doug who lays his arm round Thomas "" Thank you I am very proud of it " .

" Would you like a tour off the place Doug asks about time Darian thought it might give him an idea of what his other club would look like whenever he gets round to sorting that out sometime soon " " That would be good yes " . Darian looks at Cameron raising his eyebrow just don't be rude. That's all Cameron wanted no harm in taking a walk round the club he thought .

" HELLO JUST ME " MALCOLM shouted coming into Sam and Geraints house " In the kitchen " Sam shouted Malcolm came through Sam was half dressed just a pair joggers on no shirt he had the microwave on kettle on and was making a sandwich " Do me a favour and check on the soup please " Malcolm went over to the microwave opening it up and checking on the soup which was nearly ready . " How's Geraint " " Doing ok sounding better did Darian and Cam get to Eden club " .

" Yes they did " Sam seemed a bit stressed Malcolm thought probably because of Geraint`` Nathan got Philip " . Sam sighed hands on his hips thinking Malcolm was watching him for a second he must be tired Malcolm thought .

" Yea he's keeping him overnight. " Sam checked his phone for any updates from Geraint. Sam sighed again. Malcolm shook his head. He needed to chill a bit. He thought Maybe a good night's sleep is what Sam needs .

" Cmere " Malcolm turned Sam to face him and flung his arms round Sam's shoulders Sam leaned his head on Malcolm's shoulder " Sam Geraint will get better you just need to believe it " Sam nodded Malcolm was right he should not stress so much but Geraint needed him right now tears stinging his eyes .

Sam leaned into Malcolm more, his cock hardened Malcolm felt his hardness against him. He moved away looking down at Sam's length " Shit sorry " Malcolm sniggered looking at Sam he blushed, which was cute . Malcolm moved to Sam again touching Sam's face he leaned into Malcolm's touch . " Been a while " Malcolm asked Sam nodded " Oh " .Sam blushed looking away feeling embarrassed. Fixing himself clearing his throat was really embarrassing, Sam thought .

" I better " Sam went to move to get his soup. They looked at each other again, moving closer to each other again. Malcolm moved Sam against the table, not breaking contact . " Fuck Malcolm what are we doing " They bump heads " I dont know " . Malcolm touched Sam's face then felt his lip staring at each other .

They kiss again Malcolm kissing Sam's neck he moans he's hard again groans Malcolm looks down again biting his lip looking up at Sam again grinning " Let me or we can " . Malcolm cocks his head touching Sam's face again he bites his lip Malcolm touching Sam's lip again Sam goes to lick Malcolms finger oh wow he thought that was hot .

" What about " "Shhh " Malcolm bends down looking up at Sam here Sam thought " Malcolm not here " Malcolm gets up Sam takes his hand leading him upstairs to the spare room which would be best to use Sam disappeared for a minute bringing the condoms and Lube sitting on the dresser .Malcolm stares at Sam they look at each other again not moving for a second .

Sam went over to Malcolm lifting up his shirt kissing stipping " Sam are we really doing this " Sam looked at Malcolm doesn't he want to now which is ok

i want to just for tonight he thought . " Just for tonight " Malcolm nodded moving nearer to Sam they kissed again Malcolm moved Sam to the bed he sat down .Malcolm bent to kiss Sam he hovered over him Sam looked up as Malcolm grabbed the lube he kissed Sam again then rubbing the lube on Sam's cock Sam closed his eyes while Malcolm slicked his cock with Lube that's good he thought Malcolm kissed him again pulling harder Sam leaned back closing his eyes Jesus that's so good .

Malcolm leaned over Sam licking his nipples he moaned Malcolm scrapped his teeth over Sam's nipples again pulling at his nipple ring " Malcolm " " Shhh let me make you feel good " Malcolm slicks his finger moves over to Sam again flicking his finger inside him Sam opened his legs wider better access Malcolm kissing licking his neck while he finger fucked him tingles down his back that's so good he thought Sam closing his eyes .

Sam lay on his side Malcolm's arms round him kissing his neck while he entered Sam getting into a rhythm Sam moved his ass for Malcolm to ride him harder he licked his ear kissing his ear " Harder please " Malcolm moved Sam onto his back lifting up his ass a bit Sam panted moving his head slightly they kissed . Malcolm moves gently inside Sam holding onto his back Sam whimpered again Malcolm getting into a rhythm again . " Oh god that's good right there " Malcolm held onto Sam riding him moving together Sam shouted Malcolm held his mouth so he wouldn't scream they were both close to coming .

" I'm gonna Cum " Sam exploded onto the bed he bowed his head fucking hell Sam thought coming so quick Malcolm stilled when he came his head on Sam's back they both collapsed onto the bed all sweaty laying there looking at each other Sam moved closer to Malcolm he lay his arm round Sam . They kissed again Malcolm touching Sam's face they smiled at each other then Sam moved closer to Malcolm not saying anything just hugging each other .

DARIAN AND CAMERON sat at the table again they had done the tour around the club even a spa Darian was impressed and Doug his partner Thomas couldn't have been any nicer it was sickening they both thought the rooms seemed similar to Nero's even thought he had done away with the communal area Eden club had one with a st Andrews cross that's surprising Darian thought why didn't he think that another idea for the new potential club he thought .And it had been mentioned before about the st Andrews cross a possibility Darian thought .

" Another drink Love " " Are you trying to get me drunk " Darian sniggered kisses Cameron laying his hand on Cameron's knee looking at each other " You do know we're getting eyeballed " Darian didn't notice whether they were he sat up looked round at the two guys at the bar and back at Cameron he sniggered . " Whats funny" " You are babe

" .Mind you He's always stunning Cameron thought and that's ok other people ogling my man . I know he is handsome and dazzling. That's what people think when they first meet Darian .

" Hi mind if we join you " Darian and Cameron looks at the two men from the bar and motions for them to sit " I'm Stuart " " Darren " They shook hands and they offered to buy drinks which Darian and Cameron declined " Your the writer right " Stuart asked " I am we thought we would come here for research right babe " .Cameron looks at Darian and round at Stuart and Darren .

" We did " Darian smiled at Cameron " Thought l 've read your books very good " that's sweet Cameron thought a fan looking at Darian and back at Stuart and Darren " If you don't mind me saying Darian your club is top notch " Wow Darian was surprised to hear that which he thought was a great compliment. And he certainly hoped it was .

" Thank you and what brings you to Eden if you think my club is better " Darren and Stuart look at each other and back at Darian "We were curious to see " Fair enough Darian thought Cameron looked at his watch Darian looked at him " Sorry to cut this short guys our babysitter is looking after our son tonight " Cameron announces Darian looks at him yes time to leave he thought . Which is the signal to say they have had enough for tonight .

" Oh sure no problem, hopefully see you at Neros' ' Cameron took a Darians arm and said their goodbyes to Darren and Stuart. They did seem nice but it's best to go before anything else happens which wouldn't have happened anyway .

" Mr Longstrome, Mr Fraser going so soon " Inga asked when they were about to leave Darian looks at Cameron and back at Inga `` Yes the babysitter you see and thanks for having us " Darian says Inga nods he goes into his pocket bringing out a twenty pound note Inga looks surprised at the gesture . " Thank you " .

Yes indeed Cameron thought that's too generous. Maybe he thought she didn't get many tips and it made her day getting one Darian was always generous with his tips in the past . Inga looked down at the twenty pound note in her hand .

While on the drive home Darian lay his hand on Cameron's leg they looked at each other Cameron slid his hand on Darians leg and then felt a bulge he smirked Darian looked over again and back on the road until he came to an abandoned lane to park . Darian reaches over to Cameron they kiss Darian looks in the back looks at Cameron then they both scramble into the back Darian hoovers over Cameron then trying to get into a comfortable position and end up giggling at themselves . " Darian " "Mmm " Cameron reaches up and grabs him, pulling him down Cameron straddling him . " That's not fair " Cameron giggles and kisses Darian` `What isn't fair besides we agreed to verse didn't we " Cameron cocks his head and smirks .

" your amazing I love you " " love you to " Giggling Darian pulls Cameron down to him kissing him then pinches Cameron's bottom Cameron yelping.

SAM WATCHED FROM THE bed Malcolm picking up his clothes from the floor Malcolm looked up at him Sam smiled " i gotta go Sam the guys are due back " Is he embarrassed Sam thought because he doesn't have to be .

" It's fine " Sam sat at the edge of the bed Malcolm came over to him, the sheet half over him " You good " Sam nodded looking up at Malcolm " I won't say anything between us " .Malcolm touched Sam's face he wouldn't either it's just what Sam wanted Malcolm thought and its definitely just a one time thing .

" I won't either, you know I love you right " " I know "they would always have that special bond they have been through a lot together in the past Sam got up Malcolm looked down Sam was erect again he looked up at him " You can deal with that right " Sam giggled and nodded " Catch up soon ok : " Sure " .

They kissed then Malcolm left Sam sat back on the bed and winced he was sore from their lovemaking he smiled. Maybe it's what he needed. He thought he got up again going into the shower letting the water flow over him thinking about their lovemaking. Earlier years ago their sex life was good but couldn't get enough of each other back then .

DARIAN KISSED CAMERON getting out of the car giggling after they made out in the car they went into the house Frank barked from the bed Malcolm patted him that it was ok it was just dads coming home Darian and Cameron shouted they were home finally Malcolm thought that was nearly an hour ago they texted on there way back what have they been up to he thought .

Malcolm had gone to bed instead of waiting up for them. Cameron came into the room and he came over to Malcolm and they kissed . " Ok how was Sam " " Frantic as usual we had a chat " .

" good " " I texted your dad Philip is fine "

Darian came into the room and kissed Malcolm. Those two have had sex in the car Malcolm could tell shaking his head Darian cocked his head . " Did you have sex in the car again? " Darian looked up at Cameron who was grinning while stripping . " Do we need to valet it again? " .

" No we don't, it's fine right " Cameron nodded then went into the bathroom for a shower " Are you ok you're looking flushed " Darian asked Feeling Malcolm's head " I'm fine just a dodgy tummy maybe that bug going around " .

" Ok Sam ok " " Yea we had a talk so Eden " Darian huffed standing up getting his housecoat " I think maybe someone else should go and check it out " . Darian sighing he just couldn't find anything up with the club, maybe it was their appearance Darian thought .

"Why " " Not sure i think this Doug guy is dodgy and didn't want us to see anything "

Frank barked at getting up, he needed to pee. Malcolm thought he got up while Darian had his shower. Cameron went downstairs to the office to do a couple chapters of his book getting a coffee before he got settled.

Malcolm opened the patio door to let Frank out watching him from the patio door Darian came into the kitchen looking over at Malcolm and Frank . Darian got a drink from the fridge going over to Malcolm them both watching Frank run around the Garden .

Chapter 11

❝ Sure we can do that Darian, it's no problem " Marcus said while on the phone to Darian Raymond was making breakfast he looked round at Marcus coming into the kitchen while on the phone to Darian Marcus pinched Raymond's bottom he batted Marcus away shaking his head looking round at Marcus again smirking .

Marcus came off the phone going over to Raymond pinching his bottom again " Marcus " " What can't I pinch my husband bottom " Marcus wrapped his arms round Raymond kissing his neck " Did you get enough last night " Raymond giggled " Mmm " Raymond turned round cocking his head they looked at each other " What did Darian want " .

" Asked if we could check out Eden club and report back it seemed fine when they went maybe they didn't pick on anything " Strange Raymond thought yea maybe to do with a Darian going he thought " Ok we can do that " They kissed again then Marcus left to go for a shower leaving Raymond to do the dishes .

SAM CHAPPED THE DOOR and came inside for his daily run with Cameron he heard talking coming from the kitchen and went in Nathan was there he had brought back Philip from his sleepover Darian was with Cameron at the breakfast bar . " Sam " He looked up at Malcolm coming downstairs " Run with Cam " Malcolm got closer to Sam he looked into the kitchen " You ok " Malcolm asked smiling at Sam " Yea fine talk later ok " Malcolm nodded then picked up his rucksack for college he rubbed Sam's arm smiling at him Sam nodded again let's not make it awkward Sam thought .

" There he is " Cameron laid his arm round Malcolm's shoulder "Sorry i'm late, was talking to Geraint " " is he ok " Malcolm asked looking at Cameron " Yes i'll go see him later antibiotics help " . " That's great Sam " .Cameron was pleased to hear Geraint was doing better and Sam had been worried a lot .

" Ready " Darian asked Malcolm he nodded he picked up his keys he was going to the club deliveries today Darian kissed Cameron before they left Sam stared at them before Darian and Malcolm left he would drop Malcolm off at college .Sam chewed his lip miles away he didn't hear Cameron and Nathan's conversation .

" Right i'll get Frank's lead Dad is gonna give Philip his bottle while we have our run "Cameron looks at Sam he seemed miles away he thought " Sam looks at Cameron and Nathan " Sorry What did you say "

" Dad will look after Philip while we have our run " " ok " .

CAMERON LEAD FRANKS lead out a bit more while they ran round the block via the park so Frank could get a run around before they got back home Sam drank his water while they waited Cameron looked at him " Your doing ok right " Cameron asked Sam looked at Cameron he nodded while Frank still sniffed around the grass . " just a little stressed regarding Geraint " That's understandable Cameron thought Malcolm did mention he was Cameron patted Sam's shoulder " We're here for you Sam " " That's what Malcolm said " .looking round at Cameron everyone was being helpful regarding Geraint which is great he thought I should be Thankful for friends that care .

Sam's phone rang it's the hospital phoning he's not long off the phone from Geraint he connected the call to them " Hello " " it's me I asked to use the phone my charger Sam " Jesus Sam thought he nearly had a heart attack shaking his head " " Geraint seriously " Geraint sniggered Sam told him off for that . He would have got him a new one if needed . Geraint apologised for calling him on the hospital phone while on their way back to the house .

Malcolm opened the car door Darian touched his arm Malcolm looked round at him " What " " No kiss " Darian pouted Malcolm smiled shaking his head reaching over to give Darian a peck on the cheek " Is that all " " For now " Malcolm gets out the car bends to lean on the window " I love you " Malcolm says first " love you to " Malcolm stands up watching Darian drive off smiling day dreaming the. Thought about him and Sam and last night .Fuck Malcolm thought I feel kinda bad about it but it's what Sam needed last night .

" Wow man nice car " Malcolm looked round at Blair checking out Darians sports car " Yep he likes his cars " Malcolm and Blair walked up the steps to go into college " Are you coming to julianne's party the weekend " "Not sure yet " Blair looks round at Malcolm " Ok that's fine it be great to meet Darian and Cameron "

What Blair means is Malcolm thought that everyone is curious to know about their relationship which isn'tTheir business Malcolm thought he liked his college friends but sometimes they ask too much Jenny wasn't like that . He kinda misses her now there daily stupid chats he will message her soon to catch up .Even though his other college friends were ok just sometimes Blair could be too over the top about certain things .

NEIL MANAGED TO GET a new sofa for half price at one of the charity shops which did delivery's and a few other essentials for the flat he moved around things see how they would look until it was perfect the door chapped Janet came inside what a difference the flat was she thought it was looking good which she was happy about . "What do you think? ""Good , glad you managed to get some bits, the couch looks great " Janet pointed over at the couch. Neil looked around, checking it out, maybe other bits he could get soon .

" It does " " I've done the Rotas check later " Janet sat down on the couch comfy she thought Neil watching her "How is group therapy going " " Good there a good bunch thanks for the recommendation " Neil liked the group he felt comfortable with they were a good bunch he thought .

Janet was pleased to know that her son when he was living went to the same group therapy and the same two people ran it. Neil had been going a couple times and felt comfortable with the group since the last group therapy didn't work out sometimes after they would go for a coffee or just after hanging around to chat before going home which was great for everyone .

" NEIL I WANTED TO TALK to you about something " " Sure what is it " .

Janet sat down on the couch. Neil looked at her and she seemed kinda sad. He thought " Our son's birthday is tomorrow if Roy is grumpy you know why " Neil did wonder why Roy was a bit grumpy. It must be hard for them, he thought, since he was their only child .He felt sad for them after all the years, it's something they have not gotten over yet .

" Also we were thinking of extending the cafe ". " where to " .

Janet explained their upstairs flat they could use would be big enough they had looked at another Flat that was up for sale across the road but would just be an idea for now till they decide for definite they would have to check out finances first . Neil thought it would be a good idea even though the others would have to be on board to which they didn't think would be a problem. It would be good to give the coffee shop a bit of DIY some new paint and Janet had a look at other stuff she could get for the Coffee shop .

Neils phone beeped of an alert which was his time to get to group therapy " Neil you do know you can talk to us to " " I know " Janet took his hand he was really grateful for this new chance Janet reaches out to Neil to hug him patting him on the back giving him words of reassurance.Which Neil was grateful for and letting Janet and Roy giving him the flat to .

MALCOLM AND SAM MEET after college which they normally did Sam had been to see Geraint earlier Malcolm sat down there with two cokes and went back to get their order he looked over at Sam on his phone which he was engrossed at and wondered if he was ok about everything he wouldn't push it see how he was first. He very much wants to lose Sam's friendship; they were best buddies for life, that's for sure Malcolm thought .

Malcoln sat back down looking at Sam eating his burger while still on his phone avoiding him he thought " Sam " Sam looked round at Malcolm " Mal im fine what happened you did me a favour " " Good and your Sure " Malcolm smiled Sam nodded thank god for that he thought " Geraint ok " " Getting better " . Sam said , going back to his phone, Malcolm watching him .

" Good " Malcolm touched Sam's hand smiling at him " Malcolm " " Mmmm ."

Malcolm looked up at Sam while eating his chips ` ` Could we have a boys day just you and me like we used to do? " Malcolm snorted. He looked serious. Malcolm thought they often had a day together after college or he went round to Sam's . " Of course we can know I would do anything for you , you're my best friend " .Malcolm dunted Sam's shoulder. It's been a while since they properly had a good chat about stuff .Really catch up no distractions just him and Sam like the old days Malcolm huffed thinking back on those times good and bad .

Sam grinned Malcolm looked at him shaking his head leaning into Sam " And that was just a one off Malcolm whispered into Sam he looked at Malcolm nodding " " I know that " definitely a one off Sam thought while he ate his burger grinning into himself about their night .it was a good night smiling into himself .

NEIL CAME INTO THE pub with a couple of the group therapy friends Nancy and Dan. They got their table. Neil noticed Malcolm and Sam at the far side chatting away to each other and having their meal . " What do you fancy? Neil " Nancy asked, checking the menu " Excuse me people I know " .

" Hey Guys " Malcolm and Sam looked round at Neil surprising he was looking good Malcolm thought he looked at Sam and back at Neil " Neil hey how things "

" Sam , yea I'm with a couple people from group therapy " Neil pointed to who they were Malcolm, Sam looking over " How's that going " " Pretty good and working at the coffee shop is good to I'll leave you guys to it "

Malcolm stood up going over to Neil before he went back to his friends " Neil " Neil looked round at Malcolm Sam watching " it's good to see you getting your life together " . That's kind of Malcolm to ask Neil though and he is thanks to Malcolm and Janet's help before .

Neil nodded, looked down at the floor and back up at Malcolm " Thanks" Malcolm patted his arm good on him Malcolm thought and was pleased to know he was getting on ok . " Neil left, going back to his friends Malcolm went back to Sam . ""He looks better "" Yea he is really pleased he's doing better ` ` .Hopefully he won't relapse Malcolm thought .

Sam's phone beeped of a text from Geraint Sam smiled must be a good text Malcolm thought Sam looked up at Malcolm "Missing me " Malcolm phone also beeped he checked who it was Cameron outside waiting for them to pick them up .

" Cams here " They got there and things went out. Cameron, waiting for " Mal " Malcolm, looked round at Sam " What " .Malcolm went over to Sam. Is he ok? He looked thoughtful .

" i'm gonna go to the hospital visit Geraint for a bit " " Ok " They hugged watched by Cameron he smiled at there interaction then Sam left to get a taxi for the short distance to the hospital .Malcolm got into the car reaches over to Kiss Cameron " Hi " "Hi " .

" Sam is going to see Geraint " " is he ok " Cameron asked looking out the window he would have driven him to the hospital Cameron thought but I guess he wants to make his own way there which is totally fine Cameron thought .

" Yea fine " Cameron drove off Malcolm turned on the radio "Whams I'm your man came on" Malcolm looked at Cameron smirking. He looked round at Malcolm staring at him " what " " nothing just like looking at you " soppy sod Cameron thought driving along the road home taking Malcolm's hand they hummed along to the wham tune on the way home . They both liked some of the 80s music which was Darians era; they had often teased him about that .

SAM STOPPED LOOKED at a Geraint for a second in bed he looked up at Sam standing watching him " Hey you " Sam came over to Geraint kissed him then hugged him " Hey what's up " " Nothing you said you missed me so I came " Sam sat on the bed beside Geraint he touched Sam's face they looked at each other " I was bored " Sam snorted shaking his head . " Babe you can't be bored you have your iPad and a couple magazines "

" I know but that's ok for a little while thanks for coming, " Sam sat beside Geraint on the bed, taking Geraint's hand, kissing it. " Need anything? " Geraint smiled, reaching his arm around Sam, kissing his cheek . " Nope you being here is enough " That's good Sam thought Geraint took out the other side of the iPod giving it to Sam to listen together . Iron Maiden Sam sat back getting comfy laying his head on Geraint's shoulder while they both read the magazine while listening to music .

Malcolm went into the nursery Philip awake gurgling kicking his feet Malcolm looked down at him " What are you up to then Mr huh you should be sleeping " Malcolm bent down to pick him up cradling Philip " Are you not sleepy " Malcolm sat down Philip on his lap looking up at his dad his little cheeks red " He's been a bit grumbly " Malcolm looked round at Lydia coming into the room " With his teeth ": Lydia explained Philip had been chewing on one his toys earlier .

Malcolm looked down at Philip. He was biting into his chew. Yep, they must be sore. He thought " Donyou wants me to take him. " Lydia asked Malcolm, looking up at her, " it's ok I'll put him down, I just need a cuddle with my boy, don't I? " .

Malcolm wrapped Philip in his blanket rocking him. He's sleepy. Malcolm thought " Are those bad teeth sore? " Cameron came in with the gel for Philip. Malcolm put some on Philip's dummy and put it back in his mouth straightaway, Philip sucking on his dummy straightaway must be helping Malcolm thought .

MALCOLM GOT UP AND put Philip back in his cot . Cameron looked down at him for a few minutes then left. Cameron went downstairs. Malcolm held his arm. Cameron looked round at him smiling pointing to the bedroom. Cameron came over to Malcolm. He touched his face then they kissed . Mmm tempting but " Malcolm sniggered his book was nearly completed Malcolm kissed him " Go on then besides I have college work to do raincheck "

" Definitely " Cameron went to go playfully slapping Malcolm's bottom before he went downstairs. I'll get him back for that Malcolm thought going into the bedroom for some quiet to do some college work shaking his head then opening up the laptop to finish up some coursework .

Chapter 12

Marcus and Raymond stepped into Eden club they looked at each other not to bed they thought Inga taking them to there table then leaving leaflets on the table the various things the club provided " Can I take your order " They looked round at the waiter whose name tag said Liam "Beer please "Same " Raymond said Liam wrote down there order looking back up at them nodding .

" Any preference " Stella " The waiter left Marcus sitting back looking around the decor. Raymond watched him. He looked at Raymond and sat forward. They held hands then the waiter came back with their drinks . " Marcus" " mmm " .

Raymond sat forward again while they looked through the menu " looks not to bad " Marcus hummed seems so he thought " Mr Wilson " They looked round at Inga holding a basket Marcus and Raymond looked at each other then another waiter appeared with a bouquet of flowers " For you Mr mccallum " Raymond stood up looked at Marcus who was grinning calla lillies beautiful he thought smelling them what a lovely thought . Raymond blushed when Marcus looked at him and he was a bit embarrassed regarding the flowers .

Inga sat down the basket and left " Marcus there beautiful " " So are you " Marcus kissed Raymond's cheek he blushed " Marcus " Raymond round Marcus giggled stroking Raymond's face " Research remember " " I know Babe " They sat back down enjoying their drinks being giggly and flirty with each other like they always are with each other .

MARCUS WENT TO THE toilet. He thought after washing his hands he was about to go back to the bar when he heard a couple people arguing it's not his business to interfere but he did recognise the owner Doug from photos arguing with a girl he handed her the phone talking to someone on the phone .The girl was cross at the person who was on the phone .

Raymond was on the phone checking stuff when Marcus came back looking pissed off. Raymond thought Marcus was gathering his things coming over to Raymond " we're leaving " " Marcus why I thought " just then Doug appeared with another guy with his arm around his shoulder talking to him .Doug and Thomas went over to the bar sitting on the stools at the bar .

" Baby I'm not sure if it's the right place for us, let's go Home " " Sure that's fine " weird Raymond thought wanting to leave all of a sudden but fine it's a bust he thought but it doesn't have to be so quick Raymond thought .

Marcus and Raymond gathered their things to go Inga was at the reception going so soon she thought they had booked a room. Maybe they changed their minds. She thought "Be sure to give us a recommendation now " Inga saying to them while they left to get there car Marcus nodded while they were leaving and got into the car and drove off .Very weird place Marcus thought had a bit of a weird vibe to it he thought he would have to ask Darian that when they see him .

" I THINK HE'S USING escorts like Neil said I heard him arguing with someone earlier I think there's dodgy business going on babe " " " So Neil was right then " fuck Raymond thought thats not good and a way to run a business to .Especially using Escorts to weird way of running things also Raymond thought .

Marcus looked at Raymond, he nodded , sliding his hand on his knee, Raymond taking his hand and kissing it " I want you " Raymond whispered, Marcus looked at him again and smirked, what's got into him is it the club Marcus thought .He was kinda Horny toto .

THEY WERE ALL HANDS kissing tearing at each other's clothes going into the flat Marcus pushed Raymond against the wall there shirts opened Marcus kissing Raymond's neck then his nipples Raymond groaned Marcus sliding down taking Raymond in his mouth he held onto Marcus head while licking sucking his cock .

THEY COLLAPSED ONTO the ground Raymond straddling Marcus licking down his chest pulling at his nipple ring opening his jeans pulling free his cock Marcus hissed Raymond taking him in his mouth Marcus reached for the lube squirting some sliding his hand round to Raymond as he arched up . Marcus got more sliding his finger inside Raymond him riding his finger Raymond flushed Marcus stuck a finger in his mouth he sucked on it .That is so totally hot Marcus thought .

" Beautiful " Marcus said while Raymond eased himself on him they held hands Raymond riding him Marcus reached up kissing Raymond his orgasm ripped out off Marcus suddenly they bumped heads his cum all over each other Raymond lay down him cumming all over his belly . Marcus reached over to him smiling at him " I love spontaneous sex " " mmm " they kissed again Marcus went to get up Raymond stopped him .

"What t is it baby " " Don't go yet " Marcus sniggered and lay down laying his arm around Raymond they snuggled into each other Raymond looked up at Marcus he kissed his cheek " I love you " " love you to " snuggled into each other on the floor .

SAM HELD GERAINT'S hand in Dr Miller's office for more test results.hopefully things could be improving for Geraint His pneumonia is clearing up which was good. Dr Miller looked up at them both and back at the computer " Dr Miller just spit it out please " Geraint said looking at Sam Dr Miller looked between the two of them
.

" Your blood count came back which wasn't good Geraint " Geraint looked at Sam " Your scans the pneumonia is clearing we can tell it's the mass that's taking a while to go another six week chemo I recommend " Geraint sighed sitting back on his chair he had hoped he would be improving looking at Sam he didn't look happy he thought . Geraint took Sam's hand and they looked at each other .

" Dr Miller you did say that it may have to have another dose of Chemo. It's just so gruelling. Geraint asked, looking at Dr Miller, Sam looked at Geraint again and squeezed Sam's hand to calm him .

Dr Miller was aware of that from other patients he had dealt with in the past some made some didn't but he was hopeful for the young couple they had their lives on hold because of his Cancer " I understand Geraint but hang in there hopefully we will have good results soon " .

" I hope to see Dr Miller " .

" NEIL " NEIL LOOKED round Marcus and Raymond stood he went over to them " Hey " Marcus and Raymond looked at each other and back at Neil " You guys want anything to drink " looking between them .Marcus and Raymond smiling up at Neil he looked happy they both thought .

" Coffee please " " i'll be over in a minute "

Neil made the coffees excuse himself to go sit with them at the far side to chat " So how did it go? " Marcus looked at Raymond and back at Neil again " Very strange atmosphere we thought we didn't have, " Raymond nodded .

" Who's that? " Phoebe asked Janet looking over at Neil with his friends " Friends hunny " . They looked serious. Phoebe thought it's nothing too bad she thought of carrying on with making a sandwich for her customer .While looking at Neil with his friends good looking guys she thought .

NEIL SNORTED AFTER what Marcus and Raymond told him about the flowers and the gift package. What are they trying to prove "We recorded it all " Raymond looked at Marcus surely not afterwards Marcus looked at Raymond. " Not that part babe " Thank god for that Raymond thought blushing . Lucky them Neil thought it's been at least a month since he had sex which group therapy said to try and abstain from Neil also blushed noticed by Marcus and Raymond.

" It's been a while " Marcus and Raymond looked at each other again. " It will be good for you, I guess work on yourself right, " Raymond said Neil nodded, biting his lip. Yea he's right Neil thought although it's been a bit hard at times especially when he's been feeling horny at times and had to materbate .

" we are gonna go see Darian about our findings then we can work out something " " Ok i have records of proof hidden " Raymond looked at Marcus shrugging their shoulders " Also I think there is someone else involved in the business not just Doug and Thomas " Raymond looks at Marcus now that's new he thought maybe there could be .

" Are you sure " Neil nods of course he's sure he listens to stuff even when they didn't think he wouldn't be listening in watching " Observation " Neil shut his eyes and took a deep breath Marcus touched Neil's hand Neil looked at him " Neil you don't have to go there " " Families huh " Raymond said trying to lighten the conversation.Even though him and Marcus family had there troubles in the past and still have hopefully they could work that out soon .

Marcus and Raymond left, they both invited him over to chat at their flat sometime , have a couple beers with them or a take away which Neil thought was kind of them both something to do since he just normally goes up to the flat and just vegetates there and to think too much .Or on his phone checking stuff .

Then he thought it would be good to meet someone to connect with like Marcus and Raymond had as well as Malcolm. With his husband one day he will meet someone like that. For now he has to work on himself first so that fantasy is well in the future .

Chapter 13

Malcolm , Darian and Cameron lay in bed. They had the afternoon to themselves Nathan had taken Philip out with Olivia again which was fine by them Nathan was going to take Philip to the park after taking him to see Cameron's uncle Nathan's brother Brendon who lived by himself now since his wife passed away two years ago now .

Malcolm's phone rang. He had thought about leaving it but it was the second time within half an hour. Maybe Sam calling him Malcolm reached over to fetch his phone. His uncle Mick calling what's he calling him for Malcolm got outta bed and put on his joggers to call him back going out to the landing What's going on Darian thought looking at Cameron .

" Uncle Mick " " Sorry Malcolm it's Sam he's here and in a bad way " Damn Malcolm thought he's not doing well since Geraint didn't get good results from his last test " How much has he had " " A couple here not sure anywhere else " Mick watching from the office door .

" I'm coming right over " Malcolm went into the bedroom picking up his clothes " Sam's at uncle Micks " " I'll drive " Darian said about to get up " Darian let me go on my own ok just this once please " Darian looked at Cameron who shook his head maybe he's right Darian thought let Malcolm talk to Sam on his own " Babe Malcolms right let him go on his own "

" ok you're right " He and Cameron got up also picking up their clothes from the floor Darian lay his arm round Malcolm he looked up at Darian "Call us if you need is ok " ' I will thanks " Darian kissed

Malcolm's head he closed his eyes please let Sam be ok when i go to him Malcolm thought .

Malcolm went downstairs. Frank was asleep in his bed and lifted his head when Malcolm scratched his ears on passing, collected his bike keys then left hoping that Sam wasn't too drunk ; he thought he had been doing so well lately but with Geraint's setback .

Cameron started to put back on his socks Darian sat beside him Cameron looked at him " What " " just Sam I hope he hadn't used " Cameron laid his arm round Darian he hoped to kiss Darians cheek . Frank appeared at the door and the two of them looked over at him, guessing he wanted out. Frank came over to them, Cameron scratching behind his ears .

Darian got up guessing it was his turn to take him round the block Frank jumped up at Cameron who clapped him " Alright let's go " Darian went to the door Frank looked at him and saw what's up with this dog he thought Cameron sniggered . " What is this favouritism? Frank barked, wagging his tail, then ran out downstairs. I swear that dog knows how to manipulate.

" Right I better get a couple more chapters in " Cameron got up kissed Darian he held him back for another kiss "Behave later " Cameron giggled Darian slapping his bottom " Darian get and take Frank his walk " Darian huffed then they heard Frank bark again "Ok ok i'm coming " .Darian looks round at Cameron he winks at him then leaves to take Frank for his last walk .

MALCOM PARKED THE BIKE outside Bennetts he took his helmet off and looked up at the pub his Uncle had made improvements to the place that time Darian shut him down and ever since his uncle did some renovations.which looked so much better and the clientele was much better too . Malcolm thought about that time he worked for his uncle for a while . Malcolm walked into Bennetts his uncle at the bar Malcolm went over to him " Uncle Mick " Mick turned round to face Malcolm happy to see him " Where is Sam " " In the office " Mick took Malcolm to his office where Sam was on the couch drinking some coffee that Mick made him .

Sam looked up at Malcolm, tears running down his face Malcolm. Went to him sitting beside Sam " I fucked up Malcolm " "Tell l me you didn't use Sam " Sam shook his head Malcolm looks up at his Unkle and back at Sam " I thought about it but I didn't know just got a bottle vodka then came here stupid I know "

SAM HUNG HIS HEAD MALCOLM lay his arm round Sam's shoulders comforting him " I'll leave you guys to talk " Mick left Sam started crying shit Malcolm thought he's feeling really bad laying his arm round Sam reassuring him .

" I'm scared Malcolm what if the chemo doesn't work " Sam wiped his nose this has got to stop Malcolm thought he got up poured a glass water took it over to Sam who drank it " Now listen to me the chemo will work ok you have got to get out of this funk Sam I'm serious " This won't do Malcolm thought he has to get a grip himself be there for Geraint .

Suddenly Sam felt sick and Malcolm grabbed the bucket the first thing he could think of rubbing Sam's back while he threw up " Sorry " Sam wretched Jesus Malcom. Though " it's ok " Malcolm rubbed Sam's back, retching the door-chapped Uncle Mick came in and saw that Sam was throwing up in his bucket . " Sorry uncle Mick " " I'll get Doreen to clean it up " .

Malcolm's phone rang he checked it Geraint calling him he stood up went outside to take the call " Malcolm is Sam with you " " He is Geraint I'm looking after him don't worry ok " Thank god Geraint thought when he didn't come to the hospital for his chemo session . " Geraint he's scared you guys need to talk about stuff ok " shit Geraint thought Sam said he was ok whenever they chatted he must have been bottled it up .

" Malcolm I know but he won't, did he use " " No he didn't use just drank Will call you later ok with an update " dammit Geraint thought this damn cancer he just wished he could be there with Sam right now .

MALCOLM AND SAM SAT outside on the pavement for some air Sam had drunk a half bottle of water . He was starting to look better Malcolm thought which was good " Sorry " " Stop saying your sorry or I'll punch you " Wow Sam thought he really was angry with him he looked round at Malcolm texting probably Darian and Cameron sighing shaking his head he's pissed off at me .Im pissed off with myself to feeling bad for himself drinking i've just relapsed Sam thought .

" it was all so simple back then " Malcolm looked round at Sam what the hell is he talking about he thought " I love you Malcolm I always will " Sam looked at Malcolm he smiled and nodded reaching for Sam's hand " You know I do to Sam I don't think it's the right time for you guys to think about having kids maybe when Geraint is better " .He's probably probably right Sam thought that's for him and Geraint to discuss .

" I think you're right. " He is right. Sam thought maybe it was because Malcolm had Philip and they wanted their own kid who knows " Listen to you all grown up giving advice. " Malcolm snorted. It's the college course, the psychology of it, he guessed " Sam " .

SAM TOOK ANOTHER DRINK off water shaking his head Malcolm watched him Mick watched from the door checking if they were ok they looked ok chatting and Sam looked ok he thought hopefully he wouldn't have that much of a hangover in the morning .

" There talking Darian " That's good, Darian thought while he tended to Philip putting his dummy back in . ` `We were worried about Sam " . That's understandable Mick thought he was worried too . " I understand Darian " .

" EVERYTHING WAS SO simple back then we could have "What are you saying " Sam huffed giggling into himself Malcolm screwed his nose up he doesn't know what he's saying he's drunk. Malcolm closed his jacket and it was getting cold " Cam's a good catch " . He sure is Malcolm thought smiling thinking back on their first meeting at the club his crush back then . And Darian was a catch back then so he didn't think he would fall in love with an older man .

"MUMS THE WORD BUT i.did enjoy it " Malcolm sniggered there. Tryst is jealous of him with Darian and Cameron he thought because it didn't seem so from when they all met back then " Sam it's getting cold we should go " .laying his hand on Sam's knee .Sam took Malcolm's hand looking at each other .

" Do you remember when we went to Blackpool? " Malcolm did remember when they decided to have a weekend there when they turned eighteen and decided to go there for their birthdays and had a great time then they were kids back then and had each other . . "I am very eventful for our eighteenth " .Yrs indeed it was Malcolm thought .They were just young and in love .

" THEN WE MET HIM " Malcolm got up and went over to Sam knelt in front of him taking Sam's hand looking at each other " Sam that's my husband you're talking about " Sam moved nearer to Malcolm ` ` Sorry i " . He's very nearly going to punch him. He'is drunk and spouting off about stuff .

" You need more coffee and water " " i need another drink " Malcolm playfully punched Sam's arm " You don't i'll knock you out if you do " . He will not have another drink Malcolm thought .

They bumped heads again Sam felt cold Malcolm thought we should get going soon " I'll go to a meeting will you come with me " Course I will " Sam went to stand Malcolm helped him they hugged Malcolm patted his back Sam holding onto Malcolm.

" Malcolm why don't we go there again " ' " Where " Sam lay his arm round Malcolm to steady himself going back into Bennetts `` Blackpool i wanna go back what do you think " .Malcolm looks at Sam is he serious he thought .

"What i think it's a crazy idea " Malcolm snickered shaking his head Sam stood looking at Malcolm "Won't he let you go " Malcolm glared at Sam Darian doesn't own him or tell him what to do where did all the angst come from he thought Sam's drunk saying things he doesn't mean.

" Fuck Malcolm i didnt mean that " " If you wasnt my best friend i would knocked you out " playfully punching sams arm tears stung Sams eyes damn Malcolm thought now hes upset .He went over to Sam they hugged again " Stop it " " Malcolm i love him to " .Malcolm knew that how he felt towards Darian it was a different kind off Love between them thought between them.

" I know " Malcolm always knew he had feelings for Darian too and if Cameron was in the picture maybe they would have had a throuple who knows it may have worked with the three of them they looked at each other again . " Let's do it, go to Blackpool" Sam grinned, it's something they needed to do to get away for a couple days to get Sam out of his head and not think about Cancer all time .

" I wanna go see Geraint ``Sam asked Malcolm if it wouldn't be a good idea with the state he was in but if he wants to Malcolm cant stop him." Ok we will go and see him " .

GERAINT LAID HIS ARMS out for Sam to go to him Malcolm watched them kiss and hug from the door Geraint looked up at Malcolm mouthing thank you Malcolm nodded good to see Sam and Geraint hugging even though Malcolm had given him more water before they arrived at the hospital .

" Im sorry " Geraint touched Sam's face " Its ok your frustrated im frustrated " Geraint looked over at Malcolm watching them Sam looked over at Malcolm and at Geraint " Can I stay tonight I wanna be with you " one the nurses came in with a make up bed Geraint had already spoken to the nurses about it . Sam looked upset before she left and she took Malcolm outside .

" Is he ok " " He will just need to be with his husband " The nurse leaves them. I better let them have their time together, Malcolm thought .

MALCOLM PARKED THE bike in the driveway the front door opened Cameron stood at the door carrying Philip Malcolm looked up at him Cameron looking worried Malcolm came nearer to him kissed Cameron and pinched Philips cheek " I need cuddles " Malcolm said coming inside sitting down his helmet taking Philip off him going into the lounge Cameron watching him .

" How was he when you left " " Feeling rather sorry for himself " I bet Cameron thought it's something else that Sam Cameron thought but it's his business he will tell them when he's ready . Cameron came over to Malcolm laying his arm around him Malcolm looked round at him " I love you " Cameron touched Malcolm's face they kissed Malcolm leaned his head on Cameron's shoulder.

" They will be ok babe " " I know they will " Malcolm sat got up putting Philip in his basket looking at Cameron `` Did you get more done " " A bit was on the phone to Arthur for a half hour about a book event he wants me to go to " Malcolm went over to the fridge bringing out a can bru taking a drink of it . Looking round at Cameron at a book event he thought Cameron always likes to do these sorts of events .

" Sam and I are gonna take a couple days away to Blackpool it to him good " " Good idea " Malcolm went back over to Cameron looked at Philip asleep " it was our first weekend away when we turned eighteen everything is just to hard right now for him " I understand " why is he so understanding about all this Malcolm thought that's just Cameron he's different from Darian . I don't deserve those to Malcolm thought but then thought I shouldn't think like that we have a good life and having there an has been the best thing to happen .

" I'm gonna go for a shower I'm bushed "

AFTER HIS SHOWER MALCOLM got changed into his Pjs and went into Philips room to check on him he was asleep he looked round at Darian standing at the door hands in his pockets watching him . " Your home early " Malcolm came over to Darian laying his arms around his shoulders`` looking up at Darian.Malcolm gave Darian a kiss Darian snaked his arms round Malcolm .

" I was worried Jake and Claudia will be fine " Malcolm sighed he always worried he thought " Darian no need to worry we talked he had a slip up " Malcolm moved to go into the bedroom Darian stopped him Malcolm looked up at Darian again . " What " " Cameron mentioned Blackpool " .

" Darian Sam's going through stuff right now he just needs time away I don't want to fight about this' ' Cameron heard their conversation from the landing he has to stop this inquisitiveness all the time and let Malcolm and Sam do their thing . It's what Sam needs right now; he's ok about the two of them going away for a few days .Darian just needs to accept that and not be so bossy around Malcolm .

" I don't want to fight either sorry " Darian went to hug Malcolm he had to understand what other people were going through. Malcolm thought they parted and kissed " I'm going to bed " Darian nodded. " Love you " Darian said " Same " Malcolm went into the bedroom going over to the bed and getting in picking up his phone to check it Darian went to see Philip who was asleep Cameron was right his little cheeks were read from his teeth coming in .

CAMERON WAS IN THE office on his computer writing a chapter when Darian came in he wrapped his arms round Cameron he looked round at Darian " ok " Darian nodded. Leaning against the desk " I've overreacted again haven't I " Cameron snorted his usual he thought "Yes you have as always " Cameron cocking his head at Darian .

Darian sighed he couldn't help the way he was overbearing with people. Cameron lay his hand on Darians knee. He looked down at him and bent to kiss Cameron. " Now let me finish this chapter ok, " Darian nodded. Frank sniffed around their feet. Cameron went into the drawer for his treats giving him a couple of them. Frank barked at Darian , shushing him .

" Shh you'll wake Philip " Frank panted. They guessed he wanted out. Darian got up and parted his knee for Frank to come with him to let him out .Frank panted just as Darian opened the study door and Frank ran out to the kitchen .

Darian opened the patio door Frank looked up at him Darian sighed shaking his head " Go on then it's not that cold " Frank ran out to the garden did a sniff about he better not do a number two Darian thought then Frank cocked his leg and did a pee thank god Darian thought . Frank had another sniff around then came back inside going over to his bed Darian clapped him then Frank settled down it won't take him long to fall asleep .

MALCOLM WAS HALF ASLEEP when Darian came in he looked over at Malcolm dozing Cameron will at least be an hour with his writing Darian went into bed went over to Malcolm kissed his cheek " Love you " Malcolm turned round snuggling into Darian " love you to " Malcolm opened his eyes looking at Darian he touched Malcolm's face they kissed Malcolm snuggling into Darian . Darian kissed his head " Don't worry too much about Sam ok " Malcolm turned to Darian Darian touched Malcolm face " I do worry Darian " .

Malcolm moved over to Darians side leaning on his shoulder Darian lay his arm around him kissing his head " I know go to sleep " Darian said Malcolm looked up at him then leaning his head on Darian shoulder Malcolm drifted off to sleep his arm lying on Darians stomach .

Chapter 14

Raymond opened the door to Neil waiting and came inside the flat Neil gave Raymond some beers for them " Marcus is making the pizzas " "Oh right Marcus appeared from the kitchen his covers covered in flour " Thought i'd make the pizzas there nearly ready " Marcus smiled looking at Raymond he nodded and then went back into the kitchen .

Neil and Raymon went into the lounge some nibbles on the table Raymond handed Neil a bottle " it's Non alcoholic cause your off it that ok " " Great thanks "

Marcus appeared with the pizzas, onion rings and chips. If they wanted any they went all out. Neil thought of tasting one of the pizzas which was very good. He thought Raymond Sat beside Marcus while they ate and chatted about most things . Neil didn't have this kinda interaction with anyone like this for a long while it was kinda freaking him out but at the same time he was making his life better for the good he hoped and it was good that Marcus and Raymond were making an effort with him .

" Great pizza Marcus " " Thanks " Marcus looked at Raymond touching his knee Neil noticed their interaction. And thinking I want that someday and hopefully someone more his age too . Neil smiled as he looked away blushingly noticed by Raymond . " Neil Sorry did we embarrass you " Raymond asked Neil looked over shaking his head blushing again .

" No it's fine just you know with the therapy " Raymond looked at Marcus and back at Neil " Not much action " Neil picked at the label

111

of his bottle nodding Marcus got up collecting the dishes taking them through to the kitchen and bringing more beers . " you need help with the dishes " "No it's fine mostly done " Marcus handed Neil his beer and sat down beside Raymond again taking his hand looking at each other .

Neil got hard shifting in his chair " Honeymoon have you guys thought about that yet " Marcus and Raymond looked at Neil and each other again "Well we did have an idea about Ibiza for our Anniversary right babe " Marcus said touching Raymond's leg he smiled Neil wondered why not now rather than later .

" Why wait " "We want our business set up first we're planning it out first "

" That's good " There hand touching was getting to Neil the way there looking at each other Neil bit his lip trying not to make it to obvious how it was affecting him Raymond looked over at Neil cocking his head at the way he was staring at them Marcus sat back in the couch arms behind the sofa to see how this was going to play out . Raymond looked at Marcus he grinned at him looked back at Neil Raymond got up went over to Neil he sat his beer down took Neil's beer sat it down to .

Raymond went nearer to Neil what's happening here Neil thought looking at Raymond then Marcus " I didn't come here for that " Raymond looks round at Marcus looks at Neil "We know that just tonight if your up for it " Neil gulped oh wow he thought are we gonna have a three way I could be down for that could help my dry spell he thought besides he had plenty threesomes before .

Raymond kissed Neil, responding Marcus watching them from the couch Raymond lifting up Neil's shirt kissing licking his nipple Neil groaned. Marcus bit his lip. It was the most sexist thing he had ever seen. He touched himself while Raymond and Neil kissed again . Neil looks over at Marcus watching while groping himself he smirks Raymond looks over at Marcus he lays out his hand for Marcus to come over . Marcus stands up Raymond looks up at him Marcus sits beside Neil Raymond over at the other side they reach over and kiss Neil watches then look at Neil then all three kiss and grope each other .

NEIL IS PANTING RAYMOND unzips his jeans springing free his cock he pulls down Neil's jeans Raymond starts pumping him while Marcus and Neil kiss Raymond takes him in his mouth fuck that's good Neil thought Raymond stops wiping his mouth looking at Marcus then Neil they stand up laying out there hand Neil stands up they lead him to the bedroom . Marcus goes over to the drawer bringing out the lube and condoms .He looks over at Raymond and Neil , Neil is at Raymonds ass he's holding onto the bedpost while Neil is eating him out nice Marcus thought while he goes over to Neil rubbing his back he slicks his finger with the lube and goes to flick to fingers inside Neil he bucks of the intrusion .

Neil stands up, turns his head and kisses. Marcus while Raymond takes him in his mouth again while Marcus fingers him. I'm gonna come soon with the two of them working for him . They get on the bed. Neil puts on the condom and eases himself onto Raymond getting into a rhythm Marcus behind kissing his neck while Neil rides Raymond he turns his head again kissing Marcus again while Raymond flicks at Neil's nipples he groans stills for a minute then gets into a rhythm again so good Neil thought .

NEIL COMES OVER RAYMOND'S belly god he didn't think he would come that quick apologising he gets off Neil Marcus gets a towel to clean Raymond he then slicks his finger with the lube he fingers Raymond Neil watching he goes to kiss Marcus neck he turns to kiss Neil tonguing each other Raymond moans . Marcus puts his hand over his mouth, his face flushed, he bends to kiss him, lifts one leg up to enter, Raymond Neil bends to kiss Raymond while Marcus rides him all three kissing each other .

It's not long till all, three come again the three of them collapsed onto the bed Raymond moved to Marcus snuggling into his neck Marcus kissed his head Neil sat up Marcus opened his other arm for Neil to go to him Neil goes over to him while all three off them start giggling it was pretty good and hot Neil thought.

Later that night Neil got out of bed they had sex one more time before falling asleep Neil picked up his clothes and went out to the hallway putting his clothes on he wax putting his boots on when Raymond appeared. " Neil, why don't you stay " " I can't, I'd like to but no " .

" Neil are you embarrassed " " No course not it was good it's just " Raymond snorted he sat beside Neil they looked at each other "Neil we have only had one threesome before which was a long time ago you don't have to worry about Marcus and i are good " .

" You have an open relationship " "No not open just sometimes when the vibe is right " Neil got up and got his jacket looking round at Raymond " Thanks for the pizza and beer " Raymond nodded then Neil left .

Raymond thought Neil ok about all this because it was a fun time before Raymond and Marcus had the old threesome they agreed to together but not lately until now .

MALCOLM AND SAM ARRIVED in Blackpool staying at the premiere inn on the North shore they stood in the room looking round it and at the bed which was only one that wouldn't be a problem right they looked at each other "We can share a bed right " Malcolm asked Sam snorted he's freaking out because of a bed which they had shared many times . Malcom dunted Sam's side and giggled. Sam tutted then sat his rucksack in the bed.Shaking his head don't be so freaked out

Sam thought Malcom Went to look out the window, not a bad view he thought of a few people around . Walking along going about their day Malcolm smiled into himself .Thinking back about the time they came when they were teenagers .

" I'll go for a shower first Sam said while he grabbed a couple things from his rucksack " " Sure " Malcolm looked round Sam disappeared into the bathroom Malcolm Goes over to his rucksack to sort out his clothes and toiletries hanging a couple shirts on the hangers he looks round at the bed smirking to himself shaking his head they have shared a bed many times but it's different now .Because of their partners not that the others would have minded it's just two friends sharing .

SAM COMES OUT THE BATHROOM joggers on no top and looks round at Malcolm sitting up on the bed on his phone with a spare pillow down the side. Is he serious Sam thought staring at him Malcolm looks up at Sam " Whst " " Malcolm seriously " Malcolm snorts patting the bed while Sam changes . Where do you want to eat? " " Anywhere you want " . Malcolm looks up at him while Sam Changes lost in thought thinking back to that time they had come together again chewing his lip noticed by Sam .

" Pleasure beach tomorrow " Sam asked Malcolm nodded then got up to have his shower leaving Sam to check his phone a couple messages from Geraint and Cameron he will visit Geraint while they are away . That's really good of him Sam thought which pleased Sam even though Geraints family would visit.

Cameron was kind that way, always looking out for others, which was great, Sam thought that's why he liked him straight away when they first met .

GERAINT IS CHECKING his phone replying back to Sam who had got to Blsckpool an hour ago he and Malcolm were getting changed to go out and do the pleasure beach tomorrow which pleases Geraint it'll do him good to get away a few days the door chapped Geraint looked up at Cameron coming inside with the pram ":Hello brought a little one to cheer you up ".

" Hi Cameron ahh that's great " Cameron sat on the chair Philip Awake in his pram so cute he was Geraint thought " Sam just texted of their arrival " " Malcolm texted to " Cameron lifted out Philip and handed him to Geraint . " Hello you " . Geraint pinched Philips cheek he gurgled Cameron sat watching their interaction and thinking he and Sam would make great parents too someday .

PHILIP GAVE A BIG GRIN Geraint noticing a bit of a white tooth that had come through "What do you have there then ":Geraint balances Philip between his legs Philip gurgles his way of talking "We reckon another ones coming through "

" Not fun at the teething stage " True Cameron thought Philip had been up a few times in the night, previously Malcolm and Darian taking turns to check on him. They will be glad when he gets all his teeth .So they could get a proper night's sleep .

"WHEN ARE YOU GETTING home " Geraint looks at Cameron and back at Philip " Not sure soon I hope but it's the Chemo I've got to do twice weekly which is a bummer " .

" It'll be worth it in the end Geraint and your goal to fatherhood to " That's true Geraint thought one day they will be fathers and once he gets the all clear then they can start making baby plans .

WAS PHOEBE IMAGINING things was Neil more chirpier than usual she thought he had been humming to himself most the morning smiley which he does sometimes he was making coffees for customers Phoebe getting juices " you've had sex haven't you " Neil glared at Phoebe then blushed carrying on making the drinks " Phoebe " .

He had sex she thought of taking her drinks to her table and Neil his " who was it " " ain't saying nothing " Neil sniggered Janet coming out the office and noticed Neil and Phoebe giggling going over to them " what's funny " Janet asked looking between Neil and Phoebe .

" OH JUST NEIL HAVING a booty call " " Phoebe "
They heard a cough behind them. They looked round at Tyler there regularly standing there shit Phoebe thought blushing. Neil disappeared into the kitchen to get an order from Roy wondering what's up with him, Neil burying himself blushing .

" Tyler your usual " " yes please oh and I'll have one those cookies are they new"
Phoebe looked down at the counter Shane one the other cooks had made, she brought one out and laid it on a plate " Shane made them " after Tyler got his order and went to sit in his usual spot. Neil came out with the orders Tyler was watching him . He definitely had a crush on Neil. Phoebe thought she thought and she thought Neil likes him so she smiled into herself noticed by Janet who was doing an order shaking her head these youngsters she thought .

Neil got a drink from the fridge to take a few minutes to breathe. Taking a drink thinking back to a couple nights ago his threesome with Marcus and Raymond which was not to be repeated even though he had a good time but once only there were great guys but he didn't want anything complicated .

Like he had said to himself before he wanted to meet someone more his age he liked Tyler but too shy to ask him if he would like to meet for a coffee sometime he bit his lip thinking about this . " Hey you daydreaming " Shane shouted while he was making scones Neil looked over at him " Nope Shane let us know when the scones are ready "

JESUS MALCOLM THOUGHT he didn't expect to get a huge portion of fish chips mushy peas at Harry ramsdens they both took photos of there meals and halfway through they couldn't eat anymore " Man I am stuffed " Malcolm sniggered he was the same even though they had one more fish to eat but couldn't Sam rubbed his belly and took a sip his coke . His phone beeped a picture message from Geraint he opened a picture of him and Philip when Cameron went to visit earlier Sam smiled and was noticed by Malcolm .

Sam turned his phone round for Malcolm to see cute. He thought the caption "Can you see my first tooth " He's growing so fast " Sam nodded then looked Sad Malcolm touched his hand " Hey don't worry it'll happen " Sam nodded and smiled " Right I guess we better go hit the town " .

" Yea but not out to late since we have the pleasure beach tomorrow " " Yes dad " Malcolm snorted shaking his head Sam smirked i'll get him back for that Malcolm thought " What about Yates bar "

" YES WE CAN DO THAT " Yates wasn't far along the road passing an Irish pub which was busy. They looked at each other. Why not just go in there? There was karaoke on Malcolm got the drinks while Sam got a table and a couple people were up singing Malcolm came back from the bar the pub was busy but not too busy which was good. They heard a few accents, some Irish , English and Scottish. Everyone seemed ok with each other chatting away to each other everyone was friendly to .

The Dj guy did a couple songs to Malcolm and Sam thought " Aren't you both going to sing? " The lady in the next table asked if they looked round at her and could tell from her accent she was also Scottish . " Afraid not " Sam said they seemed like a nice couple. They thought it turned out that they came from Clydebank and were here with friends and staying at the seabank hotel along the road .

The golden oldies hotel Malcom thought " Are you both " Evie asked looking between Malcolm and Sam Malcolm sniggered " Best friends " Sam said bringing out his phone to show Evie a photo of Geraint " That's Geraint my husband he's going through Chemo right now " .Poor soul Evie thought Sam looks sad about it she thought .

" Sorry to hear that " Malcolm brought his phone out to explain who Darian , Cameron and Philip were " Oh cute my nephew is gay so it's not a problem he has a partner to " Bringing out her phone to show then her nephew yes good looking Sam and Malcolm thought .

WHAT A LOVELY WOMAN they thought and their friends to chatting away until they decided.to move on to another bar Yates along the road

Thought and her group of friends later Sam and Malcolm went to Yates for a couple drinks. It was after midnight when they decided to go back to the hotel since they were going to the pleasure beach and some shopping .It's been a good day so far they both thought and were glad they could get away for a few days .

WHILE IN BED SAM TURNED to Malcolm he was half asleep Sam smiled looking at his friend " I've had a good time so far " Malcolm looked round at Sam " It's been good " Sam lay on his arm Malcolm faced him looking at each other Sam got a hard on and moved slightly Malcolm sniggered . Sam blushed and sniggered too .

Sam moved nearer to Malcolm looking at each other again Sam bent to kiss Malcolm bumping heads again he slid his hand down to Malcolm's bulge Malcolm took his hand Sam carried on and slid his hand inside Malcolm's boxers they kissed again . Malcolm slid his hand inside Sam's pj bottoms both wanking each other off .Sam groaned Malcolm kissing his head while he wanked him off Sam's face flushed .

Both coming together panting then giggling there come coating there hands Sam got up went into the bathroom bringing out a towel to clean up " Sorry I " Malcolm sniggered he's feeling embarrassed which is ok " Sam it's fine let's get some sleep ok " Sam nodded chewing his lip laying the towel on the floor getting back into bed beside Malcolm .

THEY LAY BACK DOWN and Sam scoots over to Malcolm's side laying on his arm they both fall asleep eventually huddled into each other .

" NO DONT " Neil was having a nightmare hands grabbing him he couldn't tell who it was he sat up in bed his t shirt soaked with sweat he hadn't had a nightmare in a while why now he thought he looked around for his phone after 1 and lay back down the nighttime were the worst for Neil no one to help him through his nightmare which sucked . He got up going through to the kitchen into the fridge for a drink taking a glass of coke in with him back to bed he lay there looking at the ceiling taking deep breaths until he eventually fell back to sleep .

Chapter 15

❦ Are you sure this is where he is " Doug asked looking up at Dave his security " i am i saw him "

Doug thought he could see from the picture he looked happy though that's what mattered Doug thought " He also goes to a local group therapy " Doug looked up shocked but pleased to hear he was getting clean and therapy good on him Dog thought .

" Boss, where is Thomas? " " Thomas is not feeling great today. Doug got up, went into the filing cabinet and brought out an envelope, giving it to Dave. He looked up at Doug . " Boss what's this' ' .

" your fee " " Boss i was doing you a favour " Doug sat down on the envelope on the table going back round to his chair " what do you want me to do next " ..

" just observe but keep your distance "

Doug didn't want to interfere with Neils life, he wanted to better himself and quite rightly so he thought he was a good kid. He wishes him well whatever he does in the future .

NEIL CAME OVER TO ONE of the tables the regulars gave them their order. Neil noticed the car again. Is he being followed or is it Doug making sure he's ok? He didn't know Janet noticed today Neil was a bit distant today and wondered if he was ok or maybe wait till he comes to her .

Phoebe noticed Janet looking at Neil a few times. Neil was a bit quiet today, not his usual bubbly self. Phoebe lay her hand on Janet's shoulder as she looked at Phoebe . " Hes sad today " " i know "

Neil went to the toilet. He brought his phone out and scrolled the number he needed texting Darian asking to see him. His phone rang straight away .

" Neil, are you ok? " Darian asked Neil, standing up looking in the mirror "Fne , I think Darian, the registration I sent you " .

" yes i have it i will look into it don't worry i have contacts "

After his call Neil went back out Darren was serving Tyler he looked over at Neil smiled and nodded at Neil he nodded back at him .

" Neil " he was daydreaming "Looking at Janet `` Are you ok " Neil nodded then went into the kitchen for a drink Roy looked over at Neil at the fridge Janet was right he does look sad today ." Something on your mind " Roy asked, looking round at Neil hev shook his head then went back out to clear the tables .

If only he could express how he is feeling Roy thought but not push it Neil will talk to them in his own time he thought .

MALCOLM AND SAM WERE having fun at the pleasure beach. They looked up at the big dipper and looked at each other " You want to " Malcolm asked Sam nodded and remembered the last time he threw up after which wasn't pleasant that time but he guessed it would be different this time Malcolm thought he hoped .

Malcolm lay his arm round Sam's shoulder " You won't throw up this time " " I hope not " Malcolm sniggered shaking his head wimp he thought heading to the entrance of the Big Dipper a few people waiting to get on the ride to and a few more people arriving .

Afterwards Sam bent down getting his breath back Malcolm patting his back making sure he was ok Sam gave a thumbs up he was ok then stood up " Next time I won't be going on it " Malcolm giggled looked at his watched gone 12.30 time for lunch he looked at Sam who was looking better . " Lunch " Sam nodded and off they went to one of the stands to grab a burger hopefully he will keep it down Sam thought.

" Next time you said, " Malcolm asked, munching into his burger, Sam looked up at Malcolm. What's he on about? He thought " What do you mean? "" The rides and stuff cause Darian and Cam want to go to Florida and I thought you meant there " . Right Sam thought that be good they also had talked about going to the u.s too .

They did mention years ago they would like to go there and yes once Geraint gets the all clear they could go and when Philip is older to " Yea be good " Malcolm smiled, got out his phone taking more selfies and after there lunch they went round the park checking out the other features. It had changed so much since they had both noticed which was good and for the better, more rides and eating places .

" Madame Tussaud's " Sam asked since it was still early and they planned to hit one of the gay bars tonight " Sure tomorrow we can do the aquarium and tower " so off they went to Madame Tussaud's while checking out the other shops too along the way .

They got into Madame Tussauds. It was busy with tourists. They both took pictures of each other, selfies , funny faces and afterwards on the way back they went into the shops again and bought silly things to take back home they had tomorrow to get more stuff to Sam and Malcolm thought it was hilarious some of the purchases they got .

Sam jumps on the bed dropping his bags a good day exhausting day Malcolm sniggered watching Sam while Malcolm sat his purchases into his rucksack Sam sat up " I'm exhausted " he sniggered Malcolm put on the kettle sorting the cups " look at you all domesticated " Sam giggled teasing Malcolm it was good to see him happy . Sam's phone pinged and he had sent pictures of the day he checked the message from Geraint also telling him his chemo session went ok. Sam thought good and texted Geraint back with two love hearts smiling to himself .

" GERAINT OK " " HE'S fine, loved the pics, had his chemo session today, he hopes to get home next week which would be better " Malcolm handed Sam his coffee then sat on the other side of the bed turning on the tv . " Biscuit " Sam asked, handing them to Malcolm both munching into them while they drank their coffee and watched the tv . Sam looked happier today Malcolm thought it was good to see him happy and enjoying himself. It's what he wanted for Sam and he never wants to lose him since they made the pact years ago to get clean .And be friends for life for definite .

LATER THEY ATE AT YATES then headed to one off the gay bars it was busy a mixture of male female of all ages the music was good they both thought while they pranced around dancing some people on the dance floor Malcolm went to the bar to get drinks Sam still dancing with another guy Malcolm shook his head ordered two beers . " Looks like you guys are having fun " Malcolm looked round at the guy. In a shirt, tie , glasses and jeans Malcolm smiled and nodded " Yea just having a fun weekend that's Sam he's my best friend " .

" David " " Malcolm " they shook hands Malcolm looked round at Sam talking to the guy he was dancing with " " Scottish " " yea Edinburgh you " " Essex I'm here with those lot " David pointed to his friends on the dance floor " Cool " " To be honest they brought me here didn't want to come in the first place but there trying to cheer me up " .David sighed leaning against the bar watching his friends on the dance floor .

POOR GUY MALCOLM THOUGHT while David drank his beer he didn't look like he was enjoying himself " Break up " Malcolm asked David nodded " Just this month shit sorry you don't want to listen to my rant " Malcolm sniggered it was fine it's understandable with break ups "How long were you together " " 5 years engaged a year " . Not great Malcolm thought he looked so lost and it can be hard getting over a break up .

" David c'mon. And dance with us " His friend trying to encourage him Sam came over wondered who the guy was Malcolm was talking to David went to dance with his friend "Who was that " Sam asked Malcolm looked at him " David and who was that " " Eric from Sweden here with his friends and his boyfriend " Sam nodded and waved at them they seemed ok he thought .

Sam took a sip of his beer while he and Malcolm sat on the stools talking " I'm so sorry about David " They looked round at the female who spoke to him " i'm Danielle " " Thats ok im Malcolm, Sam " .Danielle smiled looking between Malcolm and Sam .She looks over at her friends over in the corner and looks back round at Malcolm and Sam .

" Great to meet you, yes it's been hard for him but we're helping him through it. He seems to be having a good time. " They look round at David with his friends dancing in the far corner now he seems a little more happier and joining in what his friends were doing while Malcolm. And Sam watched .

Malcolm and Sam went back up to the dance floor bumping each other both flinging their arms around each other bumping heads together they looked at each other then kissed bumping heads again is it the atmosphere or just being away for the weekend that there attraction to each other is strong again they were not sure about . Hopefully it's nothing too serious between them, they both thought .

They went to the toilet with hardly anyone there and went into the cubicle Sam leaned against the door looking at each other Malcolm went into his wallet bringing out a condom . Malcolm looked at Sam shocked, biting his lip. " I uh " Malcolm went nearer to Sam, unzipping his jeans. He looked down grinning and looked back up at Sam looking shocked he bit his lip Malcolm touched Sam's lip he sucked on Malcolm s finger that's hot he thought staring at each other .Fuck me Malcolm thought while grinding into each other kissing .

Malcolm bent down Sam looked down are they really doing this here not that they haven't before he thought Sam bit his lip he groaned Malcolm looked up grinning pulling down Sam's jeans he licked down his shaft Sam closed his eyes going with the feeling holding onto Malcolm's head him taking him in his mouth fuck this is good Sam thought but so very wrong to .But exciting at the same time while Malcolm sucked him off .

" Shit MalI " Malcolm stood up they kissed Malcolm kissed Sam's neck sliding his hand down stroking Sam " Malcolm " Malcolm put his hand over Sam's mouth while he wanked him off he groaned shuddering again Malcolm kissing Sam's neck his chin while he still carried on wanking Sam off . It wasn't long till he came he leaned his head against Malcolm's shoulder getting his breath back.

Malcolm opened the cubicle door got out going over to the sink to wash his hands Sam fixed himself Malcolm smirked looking at the mirror at Sam fixing himself Sam came over to him leaned against the sink " Can we go back now " Sam asked Malcolm looked at him in the mirror again he checked the time it was only eleven yea I think we've both had enough now . " Sure we can go now you ok " Sam was tired today but they still had a good time " Yea fine just tired " .

THEY WENT OUTSIDE AND noticed the David guy on the phone disconnecting his call and seeing Sam and Malcolm. Leaving " You guys going so soon " "Yea pretty tired from today aren't we " Malcom said Looking at Sam just before they left David touched Malcolm's arm he looked round at him . " I think I kinda made up with my ex " " Cool good luck " David nodded and smiled " Thanks he called me to talk so hopefully we can sort it out " .David beamed he looks down shuffling his feet then looks back up just as Malcolm and Sam walks off nice guys he thought .

" David c'mon karaokes starting " David's friend shouted from the door he looked round at Malcolm and Sam " nice to meet" " you to " Sam said then David left Sam looked at Malcolm " he seemed ok I hope he sorts it out with his ex " " I know c'mon let's get go" .

WHEN THEY GOT BACK to the hotel they took a shower together Malcolm pinned Sam against the tile for another make out session kissing each other all over Malcolm held one of Sam's up bending to lick and suck his nipples Sam groaned grinding into each other . Sam turned Malcolm flicked a finger inside him, one arm around his chest licking his neck Sam leaned against Malcom. While he finger fucked him . " Mal I'm " " Come then " Malcolm whispered in Sam's ear Sam stroked himself and it didn't take long for him to come .Fuck this is so bad n many ways Sam thought if any the others found out what they were doing they would be furious .

Sam pushed Malcolm against the tile going down on him, licking and sucking his cock he looked up at Malcolm watching him, then he flicked a finger inside him while sucking him off. And within minutes Malcolm came to Jesus . That was amazing. Malcolm thought Sam stood up wiping his mouth. Malcolm looked at him and kissed Malcolm, tasting the saltiness from him. Sam smirked, Malcolm pushing him against the tile, and they kissed again .

AFTER HE COLLAPSED onto the bed after there lovemaking Sam looks round at Malcolm he looks serious he thought Sam leans on his arm looking at Malcolm

" Are you ok " Malcolm looks at Sam " Yea fine you " " Fine I you know " Malcolm lifts his arm up for Sam to come to him "We are good Sam don't overthink go to sleep ok " .

" I'm not just grateful that we came " ' Me to " Sam moved over to Malcolm they snuggled into each other Malcolm kissed his head Sam mumbling his sleep Malcolm didn't understand what he was saying until they both fell asleep holding each other .

LATER WHILE SAM WAS sleeping Malcolm got up and went over to the window looking out. It was just after two people still around him looked over at Sam. He was so grateful to have him as a friend they would always have that bond since they had been younger and boyfriends then . Then Darian came into the picture Malcolm smiled thinking about that time then Cameron Malcolm's attraction to him to who would have thought their throuple relationship lasted and now their son who means the world to him .

Chapter 16

Big Mike Darians security for the club came up to the Vip and whispers to him Darian stares at him and nods he excused himself and leaves with Big Mike to the office Darian looked round at Big Mike before he went into his office sighing and mad at the person who is in his office .Darian took a deep breath before going into his office .

The woman looked round at him and smiled her security guard standing at the side when Darian came further into his office " Adeline " " Darian " Adeline crossed her legs again looking over at Darian sitting down at his chair Adeline looked up at her guard and nodded he moved to the couch while Big Mike stood at the door Adeline huffed looked at Big Mike and back at Darian . Is there any need for Darians security to be here so it was only a courtesy call .

" Reason for your visit Adeline " " oh I'm so sorry for turning up unannounced at your club but I'm here to check it out again like you did mine " Adeline smirked, cocking her head. If he can turn up at my club I can do the same she thought .

Darian wasn't sure whether there was a silent partner for Eden club which he was still to find out from his sources Darian reached over for the whiskey jar pouring himself a whiskey and Adeline passed the glass over Adeline reaching to get it with her red nails vile woman he thought . " Thank you " Adeline took a sip of the whiskey smirking into her glass so graciously she thought .

" You have a beautiful family Darian " Adeline pointed to the photos on his desk Adeline cocked her head " His name is Philip " Adeline hummed staring at Darian " I would never have thought you

would become human again when my sister said I was surprised and
two husbands now a baby to " .

" It's what I wanted for a long time. I love them both and our
son is the most precious thing in the world, " Adeline hums again,
taking another sip of her whiskey. " Do you know where Neil is? "
Adeline stared at Darian crossing her legs again .Cocking her head
Darian staring at him not for me to tell her Darian thought that is
Neil's business which I won't get caught up on .

That's what she had come for information about Neil " Sorry I
don't and neither does Malcolm either " Adeline huffs looks up at Big
Mike and back at Darian " I've also heard that Marcus and Raymond
have been at my club to know anything about that " .Picking at her nails
looking at

" No I don't maybe it's another new kink for them " Adeline nods
she sits her glass on the table " can I get you anything else Adeline "
Adeline smiles pointing to Darian " my dear your very clever and no
thank you " Adeline gets up her guard to she goes to the door opening
it to Claudia standing at the door who was surprised to see Adeline
what the hell is this woman doing here .

" Ahh Claudia You're still here " Claudia smiles looking over at
Darian and back at Adeline " Yes still here " Adeline looks over at
Darian " let's go Andre oh Darian I won't say it's been a pleasure i'm
sure we will meet again " .Adeline gushes shaking her head .

" I doubt it " Adeline huffed tutted again and clicked her fingers "
Lets go Andre " Andre moves to go over to Adeline glares at Big Mike
passing him and glares at Darian to what his problem Darian thought
when they left he is being very protective towards the woman .

Darian relaxed when she left the bloody woman. It was a
nightmare. He thought Claudia still stood at the door staring at
Darian. He looked up when she came nearer . " Darian, why is she here?
" Darian poured himself another whiskey, drinking all the contents,
shaking his head, bloody woman, he thought .

" not sure maybe she found out i went to Eden club which she owns " Holy shit Claudia thought why did he go there she thought first she knew about that . " Claudia a favour for me " Claudia huffed and smiled " of course Darian "

AFTER CLAUDIA LEFT Big Mike went back out to the bar Darian called Aida letting her know about her sister which she wasn't pleased about. Aida explained Adeline had been causing trouble wherever she went.lately She was going to confront her about it soon, good Darian thought she would have to .

" NEIL, CAN I SPEAK to you about something? " Neil looked round at Tyler standing he had been in for his usual and had paid for his meal. Neil excused himself by going outside with Tyler Janet and Phoebe watched them go outside looking at each other grinning as Tyler was going to finally ask Neil out. Janet hoped Tyler was a nice guy and it was obvious with him coming in everyday for his lunch .

Neil stuck his hands in his pockets. It has been getting colder lately. Tyler looked down at his feet then looked up at Neil. " I was wondering if you would like to go see that new Tom Cruise movie. " Neil smiled. Tyler blushed, biting his lip . " if you want to i'll understand if you don't want to or go for a drink " .

" I'm sober Tyler and yes I'd love to go see a movie with you " Tyler smiled shuffling his feet " in fact it was about time you asked " Neil said Tyler giggled was it that obvious Tyler thought smiling Neil was staring at him .Thank god I finally got that out Tyler thought .

Janet looked at Phoebe and looked promising. She thought they looked like they were exchanging nos then Tyler left Janet and Phoebe went to clear up dishes when Neil came back inside he noticed that they had been keeping busy with watching him and Tyler he giggled into himself shaking his head carrying on what he was doing .Neil was glad that Tyler finally asked him if he didn't he would have asked him smiling into himself .

Neil went to go and see and order Phoebe came rushing over to him " Well " " Oh we're gonna go to the cinema " Phoebe squealed and hugged him holy shit he thought " About time " Neil giggled yea he thought so to even though he was going to ask Tyler if he had wanted to meet up sometime .

" So when's the big date? " Janet asked, coming into the kitchen " Weekend going to see a movie. Janet was pleased to hear that Tyler was a nice guy who deserved someone in his life Janet patted Neil's back god they don't need to make a big deal about it Neil thought .

Neils phone pinged of a text he checked which was from Tyler Neil smiled he's so sweet he thought and replied back with smileys and confirming the times off the movie which was good off him Neil thought .Of course he would have checked but that's ok that Tyler checked first .

Another text came through from Darian to come see him at the club he had news for him Neil replied back he would come over when finished at the cafe Darian replies not to worry when he can . Neil thought he wasn't as bad as he thought Darians, a nice guy once got to know him .A pussycat Malcolm had said previously.

SAM AND MALCOLM FINISHED their shopping. They got some rock silly hats and t-shirts . After lunch they went back to the hotel to pack for going home in the morning. They both just managed to get their purchases into their bags. Sam went for a shower Malcolm thought they needed to chat about stuff before going home tomorrow. He heard the shower turn off after Malcom Though then they could talk Malcolm went into the bathroom Sam was sitting on the edge of the bath towel round him his head hung Malcolm stood for a moment. Is he ok? He thought Sam looked up, wiping his nose .

Malcolm went to him bent down in front of Sam " Sam what's wrong " " Must being silly it's been a good few days and well it's " Malcolm reached up to hug Sam " I know it's been great we should do this more often " Sam sniggered they looked at each other " A couple days away I mean " Malcolm cocked his head smiling at Sam .What is it he was meaning he thought because it's just two friends who care for each other I do love him as a friend that wouldn't change Malcolm thought .

Malcolm got up sat on the toilet seat they looked at each other " I know what you meant we put it to bed right " Malcolm nodded holding out his hand for Sam to take " its helped right " Sam nodded it sure has not to think about hospitals how Geraint's feeling worrying about his course and the baby situation if he didn't Have Malcolm he would be lost and not sure what to do .

" We both have been busy with stuff lately Sam but I promise when we get back we touch base regularly ok " Sam nodded they hugged again that would be good Sam thought .Am i still in love with Malcolm still Sam thought or is it a different kind of love between them i love my husband Sam also thought i'm just thinking about stupid stuff now .

" Fancy a take away or we could order from the menu " Malcom. Suggested that be a great idea Sam thought getting up going through to get his joggers on Malcolm following him through " Sam " " mmm " he turned to Malcolm just as he was about to change Malcolm went under the towel to feel him Sam was erect Malcolm smirked raising his eyebrows . Sam grabbed his hand. Jesus he's just had a shower he thought .

Malcolm went closer whispering " You can do the rest right " Sam looked at him then Malcolm disappeared into the bathroom. To shower Sam groaned great if got a raging hard on now shaking his head pulling on his joggers and shirt laying on the bed checking his phone .

Malcolm came out of the bathroom a few minutes later leaning on the door checking Sam smiling thinking did he or not Sam looked up shaking his head when Malcolm came out the bathroom going over to his clothes . " That wasn't fair you know " Malcolm looked round at Sam he was mad at him Malcolm went over to Sam sitting beside him . " I'm sorry " patting his hand Sam smiled, shaking his head " you're forgiven " .

Sam bumped him both giggling Sam leaned his head against Malcolm's shoulder Malcolm patted his back " c'mon lets order our food ok " Sam nodded and looked up at Malcolm going over to the table taking the menu to check .

NEIL CHAPPED DARIANS office door he heard him say come in Neil opened the door and went inside Darianon the phone Cameron on the couch on his computer he looked up and smiled Neil went over to the chair at the desk . " How are you Neil " Cameron asked Neil nodded " Fine thanks " Cameron nodded looking at Darian .

Darian came off the phone to his contact and looked up at Neil "Are you ok Neil " Fine where is Malcolm " . Neil looked round the office then sitting down looked up at Darian him.looking at Neil

" Be back tomorrow he and Sam went to Blackpool for a few days " Cameron explained. Neil thought looking back at Darian it would be great to get away for a few days somewhere. " Do you know Adeline? " Neil looked up at Darian again. He had heard that name before in the passing .

" Adeline I've heard that name is she " Darian looks at Darian and back at Neil "Apparently she is the silent owner of Eden and how i dont know she knew we went there " . Probably contacts off hers Neil thought no surprises there he thought .

" Doug i expect " Darian looks at Cameron and back at Neil " I have people checking Neil " .

Neil thought that was a good idea. His phone beeped. He checked and smiled . Tyler Darian noticed Neil looked up, looking between Darian and Cameron, " I have a date Saturday." Neil blushed thinking about Tyler; he was so sweet And excited about their date .

" Good on you Neil isn't that great Darian " Darian hummed looking at Neil " Where did you meet " " He comes into the coffee shop " that's cute to hear Cameron thought and this Tyler sounds nice also " Do you need a lift home Neil " Darian asked that's kind of him Neil thought " Thanks but I can manage back " Neil got up Darian got up going over to Neil laying his arm round Neil's shoulder " How is group therapy going ok ":.

" Yes fine Darian ' The door chapped Bill came inside Darian looked over at him Neil looked at Darian " Bill will you take Neil home " " Darian no need " This is ridiculous Neil thought i dont need a lift back .

" Sure boss " Neil sighed, shaking his head there was no need for this he thought he thanked Darian and left Darian looking over at Cameron typing away Darian grinned watching Cameron engrossed in his computer .

Darian sat on the couch beside Cameron touching his knee Cameron looked up at Darian looking at him Cameron cocked his head smiling at Darian he sat his computer down going nearer to Darian copping a feel his bulge " Darian Longstrom get your mind off that " he kissed Darian, Darian took Cameron's hand keeping it at his crotch they kissed . " We could have a quickie so I could get one of the rooms ready " .Darian asked smirking raising his brows Cameron tutted shaking his head .

Cameron looked at Darian touching his face, he hummed , they kissed again then whispered " Go on then " Darian smiled, kissed

Cameron's nose, got up and went to his table picking up the phone Jake answers .While Cameron watches Darian looking at him smiling .

" Yes boss, sure I'll have it ready " Claudia looked over at Jake. He put the phone down and looked at Claudia. She knew exactly what he was going to say. Jake got the keys from the box and left to sort the room out for Darian and Cameron .Lucky sods he thought smiling into himself sorting out the room for Darian and Cameron.

Bill parked at Neils flat. He thanked Bill for the drive home. Bill got out with him. Neil thought it was too extreme but it was orders from Darian to make sure Neil was home safe . Neil looked round at Bill when he got to the door he waved when he got in. Bill waited for a few minutes till he got the light on then got in the car back to the club texting Darian on his way back .

DARIAN SNAKED HIS ARMS round Cameron he kissed his head Cameron hummed Darian kissed his cheek Cameron smiled snuggled in together " You smell amazing " Cameron giggled turned his head they kissed " what does my sweat smell good " Darian wiggled his eyebrows Cameron shook his head " I need to pee " Cameron got up looked round at Darian smirking at him but naked .Darian thought a lovely sight to see his husband butt naked .

" LIKE WHAT YOU SEE " then disperse into the bathroom Darian checked his phone Bill had texted him about Neil and on his way back good he thought Cameron comes back into bed laying his head on Darians chest " I've had inspiration for a scene for the book " " You have " Cameron looks up and grins oh Darian thought what they have just done he bends to kiss Cameron .

" I do hope I get dedication " Cameron sits up and kisses Darian they look. At each other " You bet " Cameron slides his hand down

Darian erect again Cameron smirks starting to stroke him Darian bites his lip letting Cameron do his thing Cameron kissing his ear , his chin while wanking him off .Darian hisses opening his legs Cameron licks Darians ear he hums while Cameron carries on wanking Darian off .

CAMERON SLID DOWN TAKING Darians cock in his mouth Darian held onto Cameron's head while he licked and sucked Darian mouth fucked him bucking arching his back until he came . Cameron looked up, wiping his mouth sliding back up. They kissed Darian, tasting himself " I love you " . Cameron said first Darian smoothing his hair " love you to " . Cameron leaned over to get the lube looking round at Darian who had his arms behind his head and looking incredibly sexy Cameron bit his lip Darian raised his eyebrows .Smirking

" What other ideas do you have? "Cameron kissed Darian then straddling him Cameron cocked his head Darian looking up at him then looked down Cameron was erect Darian licked his lips looking up at Cameron again squirting some lube on his finger .Cameron bending to kiss Darian him wrapping his arms round Cameron's waist .

Cameron stroking Darian his hand slick with lube he bent to kiss him " That's good " Cameron held onto Darians hands while he kissed his neck going down his chest and back up he then eased himself onto Darian , Darian wrapped his arm round Cameron's waist again easing up licking his nipple Cameron getting into a rhythm they kissed . Again so good Cameron thought Darian looked up at him .

Darian bucked Cameron groaning, closing his eyes he was close and so was Darian " You want to come " Darian asked " Mmm" Darian stroked Cameron he was sensitive from before Darian still held Cameron when he spilling into Cameron him coming after .

DARIAN LAY HIS ARM around Cameron kissing his shoulder he could lie here all night if he could Darian thought Cameron turned his head Darian kissed him " I'm comfy " Cameron said Darian giggled shaking his head " Ten more minutes then " Cameron smiled lifting his head kissed Darian he raised his eyebrows again and here he thought he was the one initiating sex . I'm good with cuddling " Cameron smirked lying back down. That's fine by him Darian thought, snuggling into Cameron kissing his head .

Chapter 17

Sam and Malcolm got off the Train the next day it was after two and the trains were running to time thank god they thought there would be delays from the previous day they got to the exit Cameron waiting for them to pick them up Malcolm and Sam waved on there way to him .Cameron waved back smiling and they look happy he thought which is good .it would have done them both good getting away a few days Sam looked a bit happier Cameron thought .

Malcom. Flung his arms round Cameron kissing his cheek watched by Sam so cute he thought " Miss me " " Sure did " Cameron smiled Malcolm looked round at Sam `` You guys have a nice time " Cameron asked on the way to the car Malcolm looked at Sam . " We did didn' we Sam " " What we needed i needed " .Malcolm nodded and smiled at Sam he did need the few days away and for them to talk about stuff and basically enjoy themselves .And touch base with each other they talked more last night about most things and agreed that the weekend was what Sam needed it was between them the sex part and wouldn't say anything to anyone about it .

THEY GOT INTO THE CAR Cameron driving along him and Malcolm holding hands Sam sat forward " Cameron can you drop me of at the hospital please " " off course i can " Cameron guessed he missed Geraint while away Cameron and Malcolm looked at each other Malcolm looked round at Sam he was on his phone probably texting Geraint letting him know he was on his way to see him .

When they got to the hospital Sam jumped out the car waving to Malcolm and Cameron before he went inside the hospital Then Cameron drove off home " Was he ok " Malcolm looked round at Cameron `` Yea he needed the time away " " Good and you guys talk about stuff " Malcolm nodded taking Cameron's hand again . All his anxieties and thinking about stuff when he was away and what he and Sam Talked about just went away . He was in love with the two men who gave him the freedom to be himself and now that they have Philip and responsibilities now ." Yea Sam is dealing with a lot right now " That's understandable Cameron thought he had had a lot to deal with lately .

GERAINT WAS PUTTING his phone in charge the door knocked he looked round at Sam standing at the door smiling he came over to Geraint flung his arms round Geraint's shoulders he kissed him " Hi " "Hi " they looked at each other Sam touched Geraint's face I missed this face he thought .

Sam went into his rucksack looked up at Geraint " Miss me " " always do " Geraint went to sit in the bed Sam gave him a hat and t shirt he giggled at the wording " you like " Geraint put his kiss me quick hat on Sam had to take a pic of him wearing his hat it was so cute to .

The nurse came into Geraint's room seeing his hat and giggled " nice " she said Geraint his pain killers " will you stay over Sam " " thanks not tonight got the house to sort and I have a washing to do "

SAM SAT BESIDE GERAINT he took out his phone again to show him the photos they took while away Geraint was glad he took time away for himself which he needed Sam sat up looking at Geraint " I got you a new beanie to " Sam went into the bag bringing out the beanie which had a Harry Potter emblem on it Geraint put it on . " How do

I look? " Sam gave a thumbs up then snapped a picture with Geraint doing a thumbs up

" DID YOU MISS ME MR " Malcolm asking Philip pinching his cheek Philip giggled Malcolm could see more off his tooth now and another one coming through Malcolm sat on the chair Philip on his lap Malcolm picked up his bottle " Are you a hungry boy " Malcolm gave Philip his bottle he also looked cute in his new outfit that Malcolm bought him which he wanted to do when he got home .

" Wait and see if pops like your new outfit " " I do like it " Malcolm looks up at Darian standing at the door Malcolm smiled Darian coming inside Darian giggled looking at Philips outfit my daddy bought me this lousy shirt ." Aren't you cute? " Darian said looking up at Malcolm " Hi " " Hi " Darian reached over to kiss Malcolm I've missed his face Malcolm thought rubbing noses .

" Your home early " " Wanted to be here since your back besides Claudia is able to look after the club "

" Have you had enough buddy " Malcolm stood up Philip burped good one son he thought and laid him down in his cot putting his dummy in Malcolm looked at Darian " Neil ok " " He was has a date on Saturday " That's great Malcolm thought sliding his arms round Darians waist ' that's great and the other thing " " looking into it " good Malcolm thought we don't want any problems since they have Philip now .Because Darian would do the best security anyway .

" Going for a shower " Malcolm took his arms off Darians waist he took Malcolm's arm they looked at each other " Room for another "Malcom smirked walking away he looked round at Darian watching him before he disappeared into the bedroom .Darian looks round at Philip looking down at him " Behave now little one " .

DARIAN KISSES MALCOLM'S shoulder neck while stroking him letting the water flow over them Malcom pants the shower door opens Cameron coming inside the three off them kiss Malcolm goes to Cameron he bends down taking him in his mouth while Darian and Cameron kiss fuck good Cameron thought . "Mmm, have you had another idea for your book of love? " Cameron sniggered. Malcolm stood up, sandwiched between the two, kissing both Darian and Cameron . I just may have thought Cameron thought all three of them were kissing each other .

Malcolm felt Cameron hardness against him he wiggled Cameron kissing his neck while he Guided himself into Malcolm him holding onto Darian them kissing Cameron getting into a Malcolm shouted out Darian kissed him to silence him his head on Darians shoulder while Cameron fucked him .Cameron wrapped his arms round Malcolms waist pounding into him .

ALL THREE CAME TOGETHER kissing each other while coming down from their orgasm. Malcolm thought getting dried afterwards hugging each other then Philip made his presence . ". I'll go, " Cameron said quickly, putting his joggers on .

Darian wrapped his arms around Malcolm's shoulders and they looked at each other in the mirror Darian kissed his neck " I take it you missed me " " What do you think " .

Malcolm turned to face Darian. They kissed Darian, opening the towel grinding into each other. " Darian Dont" or " Darian licked Malcolm's ear he leaned closer to Darian " Later Love " .

SATURDAY CAME NEIL just got to the cinema with five minutes to spare Tyler arrived a few minutes later " have you waited long " " no just got here " Neil smile is Tyler nodded Neil seemed a bit nervous Tyler thought

That's good Tyler thought he hadn't waited that long " i already bought the tickets " "Tyler you didn't need to' ' .

" My treat, " Niel smiled thinking that Tyler didn't need to do that. They went inside. Tyler did insist on buying the drinks and popcorn which was crazy. Neil gave him his half. He wanted to at least pay his way inside the cinema. They got to their seats chatting before the movie started .

Neil went to grab some popcorn, his hand collided with Tylers Neil blushed and stuffed some into his mouth looking away biting his lip thinking this is kinda good news to him but he was enjoying himself. This film is getting goodThey both thought they looked at each other now and again throughout the movie .

AFTER THE MOVIE STANDING outside the cinema deciding where to go and opting for Wetherspoons Tyler got himself a beer orange juice for Neil checking what to choose to eat while they both looked through the menu .

" I'm gonna have burger chips " Tyler said Neil looked up " same " Tyler got up Neil touched his arm Tyler looked down at him " let me pay you paid the cinema please " " ok " .

They ordered the meals and chatted about most things. The movie Neil found Tyler easy to chat to. " What do you do for work? Neil asked " my dad has a construction company I help out sometimes or in the office Bullman construction " Neil had heard of it before whenever passing billboards before the advertisement for the company .

" The Coffee Shop do you like working there " " I do Janet and Roy are great and have helped me out a lot "

Neil stopped, he wasn't ready to divulge in his past yet not till he got to know Tyler better he took a sip of his drink looking up at Tyler

" Tyler be patient with me that's all I ask " Tyler reached for Neil's hand he looked down at them holding hands . " We have all the time in the world Neil getting to know each other " Neil was pleased to hear that he smiled and nodded Tyler smiled back . I won't push things Tyler thought when he is ready to tell me I'll listen .

   " Are you free tomorrow " Not doing anything why "

" SPEND THE DAY WITH me, what do you think? "Sure let's do that, what do you suggest? " Tyler got up to sit beside Neil. They scrolled through things to do, then they came up with the idea that Neil had only been to the zoo once when he was younger. He liked that idea . " I'll pick you up what do you think " " yea fine " I'd love to spend the day with him Neil thought he makes me feel comfortable in his presence .

   " Are you ready to go we could share a taxi " " Sure " They went outside Tyler rang one and within Ten minutes it was here dropping off Neil first Tyler got out telling the driver to wait they hugged Tyler giving Neil a peck on the cheek . "See p you tomorrow " " See you then thanks for the movie "

NEIL LOOKED ROUND AT Tyler before he disappeared into the flat, the driver setting off to his place he quickly sent a text to Neil saying he enjoyed the company Neil leaned against the door reading Tyler's text yea he enjoyed his company too grinning I really like him Neil thought I don't want to fuck it up he thought .

Chapter 18

Malcolm pushed Philips buggy while they walked along the path at Edinburgh Zoo Sam beside him Darian and Cameron behind arm in arm they had asked Sam if he had wanted to come which he agreed to Geraint was feeling better the hospital hoped to let him home in a weeks time then go in for his chemo weekly Sam would have loved him to be with them but when he gets better they would come to the zoo .

They stopped at the monkey enclosure Malcolm bent down pulling round Philips buggy to watch the monkeys. They were noisy.. They just sat looking around. Malcolm looked round at Darian. He smiled " He looks like the king of the jungle just like you, " Darian huffed, shaking his head cheeky as Malcolm looked up at Darian smiling at him .

Philip made a noise and everyone laughed. He wanted to be heard just like the monkeys to Cameron bent down " You making a noise like them too " Cameron stood back up looking at Darian watching the Monkeys Darian giggled and looked at Cameron watching him take his hand .

Then they moved along to the other enclosures, this time Darians turned to push the buggy blowing raspberries at Philip, him giggling " are you a good boy " Darian reached down pinching Philips cheek .

NEIL AND TYLER STOPPED to look at Lions who were laying down Tyler lay his hand on Neils back Neil smiled into himself the warmth of his hand on his back . They moved along looking at the other animals Neil noticed Malcolm with his two husbands, the baby and Sam he watched them for a second they all looked good together he thought .

Malcolm saw Neil he waved when they got nearer " do you know them " Tyler asked Neil to look round at Him " School Malcolm went to the same school " " Neil hi " .

Malcolm looked between Neil and Tyler. Neil introduced Tyler to Malcolm they shook hands "Your kid " Tyler asked them going over to the others "Yea from a surrogate Philip " Tyler looked down at Philip what a cute kid he looked a bit like everyone he thought and noticed a bit of a tooth .

" Hello are you having a nice time " Tyler speaking to Philip he stared up at Tyler then grinned showing his tooth. Tyler thought they seemed nice people so he got the inkling Darian , Malcolm and Cameron were together and Sam a friend of Malcolm's.

" How's it going? " Malcolm asked, taking Neil over to the side. They looked round at Tyler, talking to the others. " Good so far he's nice, Malcolm , I haven't."Malcolm touched Neils arm, nodding " Only when you're ready Neil one step at a time ok "

Neil nodded he just didnt want to fuck it up and scare Tyler off whenever he tells him his past the things had happened to him Neil nodded Tyler came over to them looking between them . " catching up Malcolm was at Blackpool " " cool good time " .

" Sam and I went his husbands going through Chemo right now so we decided to get away few days " " Sorry To hear that "

Malcolm and the rest went off to see the penguins while Neil and Tyler went to the cafe for pit stop Tyler's phone beeped he checked a text from one his friends asking how their date was going he will text them back later he looked up at Neil watching him . " One of my friends asked how our dates were going . Tyler smiled. Neil blushed looking down at his coffee cup. He smiled at himself thinking that's nice of Tyler's friends to ask .

Tyler reaches his hand over and Neil looks up cocking his head " Going good right " " Uh huh " Tyler smiled while taking a sip of his coffee after they went round to see the rest of the animals before going back home Before Tyler started the car he looked round at Neil `` You want to come to mine I can make us something " " Sure I'd like that "

TYLER OPENED THE DOOR to the apartment just as Neil's phone beeped of a text he checked from Marcus and one from Darian " You wanna take that. Tyler asked, going into the kitchen, Neil looked up " No it's fine, just an update on something " Neil looked round the flat, a nice place he thought taking off his jacket neutral colours over at the side. Tyler had a fish tank Neil went over to inspect three fish, one a goldfish, the other two clown fish .

",Do you want " Tyler stopped saw Neil at the fish tank inspecting the fish Tyler smiled coming over to Neil he looked round at Tyler `` What are there names " Tyler pointed to each one saying there names one Angel , Loki and Thor Neil giggled what strange names to give the fish . Tyler had them for a couple years now and thought of getting a snake once but decided against it .

" Right, do you want chicken with the pasta " Oh " sounds good yes " Tyler got up and Neil got up to follow Tyler to the kitchen " Can I help " Tyler handed Neil the sauce for the pasta he had,ready to put the pasta in the pot the chicken was already diced .

Tyler went to put on some music Rag n bone Neil liked a couple of his songs from before Tyler came over to Neil looking over his shoulder on how he was doing Neil turned his head they looked at each other Tyler kissed him Neil turned to face Tyler lifting his arms up to his shoulders . Oh no Neil thought he's now got a boner and moved blushing Tyler went to him lifting his chin up . " What's wrong? " Neil bit his lip looking down. Tyler looked down and backed up at Neil .

" Sorry " Tyler snorted, touching Neil's face then kissed his nose " No need c'mon let's get this pasta sorted thank god Neil thought of helping out with the preparations because he wasn't ready to have sex with him yet .Or was Tyler he thought it's just dinner they are having right.

" WELL TYLER YOU'RE a keeper that was amazing " Tyler snorted putting down their plates. Neil took a drink, his coke, Tyler a drink, his beer " A keeper am i " Tyler asked looking round at Neil " Just t an expression " Tyler nodded grinning Neil blushed Tyler thinking he's cute when he blushes .

THEY LOOKED AT EACH other Tyler moved closer to Neil touching his face leaning into kiss Neil Tylet held Neil's neck there kisses became more frantic . Tyler lifted up Neils arm, pinning it against the couch. Neil was hard again. Tyler went to kiss Neil's neck and groaned .Tyler grinding into him shit I don't want to come in my jeans Neil thought .

" Tyler " Neil pushed him off he looked at Tyler was breathless Neil sat forward did Tyler see a scar he wasn't sure Tyler sat forward touching Neils back . " Sorry you ok " Neil nodded looking at Tyler oh god I've pushed too hard Tyler thought staring at each other .Is he ok god it's been months since I've met with anyone Tyler thought .

Tyler took Neils hand and tears formed in eyes " Tyler i'm ok " "Are you sure " Neil nodded " You have made me feel "strange thing to say Tyler thought touching Neils face he gave him a light kiss bumping heads Tyler lay his arm round Neils back .They kissed again holding each other that feels nice Neil thought .

" Stay over here tonight what do you think " " i'd like that i hate night times " Neil lay his head on Tyler's shoulder " i understand " fuck

Tyler thought what is it about night times Neil doesn't like .I will give him time to tell me himself Tyler thought .

Neil looked up at Tyler he kissed Neils head Tyler got up Neil looked up at him " i'll get you spare pjs' ' Tyler gets up Neil watching him go into the bedroom Neil sits back on the couch scrubbing his face and smiling thinking it's been a good date .And it's only staying over don't overthink it Neil thought .

ADELINE SUCKED ON HER volunteer arm. She had been coming to her for some time. Now the door knocked Adeline growled and sat up wiping her mouth, who dared disturb her feeding. She thought her young man, seeing to his wound, the door chapped again Adeline sighed Jesus' patience she thought growling her staff knew not to disturb ner feeding .

Adeline got up and opened the door to her housekeeper Blanche `` What " "Miss deline your sister " Adeline huffed looking round at Raoul sitting on the couch tending to his wound she looked back at Blanche sighing .crossing her arms what the hell does her sister want she thought .

" I will call her later. " " No you won't. " Adeline looked around. Why is her sister here? She thought coming into her lounge Aida looked over at the young man sitting at the couch he looked up . " Raoul darling can you give us privacy " Raoul got up and left Adeline and went to sit on the couch looking up at her sister crossing her legs .

" what do you want Aida " Aida flitted to Adeline grabbing her neck fangs out Adelines fangs descended growling " Threaten anyone again or you will have me to deal with " Aida let go off Adeline neck standing watching her Adeline looked up at Aida smirking shaking her head .Ahh so Darian has told her had he Adeline huffed folding her arms again hugging again .

" Eden club Adeline " Adeline huffed crossing her legs " it's just a club darling " Aida tutted going over to the drinks cabinet pouring herself a whiskey looking round at her sister . " You better tell me now or the council will be here sister "

Adeline got up going over to her sister pouring herself drink Aida looking at her " Adeline I care about you your my sister please let me help " Adeline huffed taking her drink I suppose she is right she thought it's a mess maybe the council will help " Ok ok don't badger me " Adeline looked at Aida " Thanks "

If the council gets wind then it's trouble Adeline thought besides it's not much of her problem anyway not that I had wanted anything to do with the damn club she thought Aida was standing studying for . " What is on your mind sister "

NEIL MUMBLED IN HIS sleep while Tyler had his arm around him Tyler smoothing his hair back comforting him he kissed Neil's head and moved nearer to Tyler he opened his eyes they looked at each other Tyler touching Neil's face " Go back to sleep " Tyler lightly kissed Neil he hummed snuggles into Tyler loving the warmth of him this is nice he thought someone to cuddle into at night to keep his bad dreams away .

Neil slightly snored. He was now in a deep sleep which was good. He thought Tyler was moving closer to Neil laying his arm over Neil's stomach watching him for a few seconds before he fell asleep .

Chapter 19

Neil moves to snuggle into Tyler no one there he opens his eyes no Tyler Neil sits up looking around the room where Neil thought he checked the time just after seven Tyler doesn't have work neither does he Neil gets up goes into the lounge Tyler is feeding the fish Neil shakes his head unbelievable he thought .But it's cute to see him being so tentative towards his fish while Neil stood watching him .

Tyler looks round at Neil watching him from the door " I was coming back to bed " Neil comes over bending down watching the fish feed " I wondered where you were " Neil looks over at Tyler ";I'm here " Tyler lays out his hand Neil takes out then they look over at the fish . The three of them swimming around and catching the fish food it feels kinda relaxing Neil thought .

" Breakfast " " Hmm. ": Tyler wraps his arms round Neil's waist bends to kiss him oh no not again with the hard on Neil thought he looks down biting his lip looking back up at Tyler who is grinning Neil looks down again oh he also had a hard on . " Umm sorry " Tyler goes nearer to Neil again he loves his blush " it's been six months since " Tyler said looking at Neil he looks away " Uh unexpectedly 3 weeks ago " .Neil explains chewing his lip very unexpectedly then .

Tyler takes Neil's hand he stops Tyler looks round at him he's shy all of a sudden " Neil we're just gonna shower " " Oh " Tyler giggles comes nearer to Neil touching his face " We are not doing that I behaved last night didn't I " Neil nodded Tyler took his hand leading g them to the bathroom yes he was a gentleman last night .And so was he which he found it hard at first but it was a good sleep best he had in a while Neil thought .

THEY BOTH LET THE WATER flow over them Neil facing Tyler both naked and hard they kiss Tyler moving Neil to the tile leaning against it Neil slid his hand down palming Tyler's cock he hissed they kissed Neil started to stroke Tyler he closed his eyes letting Neil do his thing feeling good Tyler thought .They kissed and nipped at each others necks Neil leaving a slight bruise on Tyler's shoulder marking his territory .

Neil moved down taking Tyler in his mouth Tyler holding onto his head while Neil nipped and sucked Tyler leaning against the tile he was gonna come soon " Neil I'm " Tyler exploded into Neil's mouth fuck me Tyler thought not to come so quickly Neil stood up they kissed Tyler tasting himself wrapping his arms round Neil's shoulder . Looking at Neil smirking, I must have done a good job when he came quickly .

" Better " Neil asked, kissing the tip of Tyler's nose Mmm" Tyler smiled they kissed again rubbing against each other Tyler kissing Neil's neck " Tyler "Mmm."

Tyler kept kissing Neil's neck " Tyler if you don't stop doing that " Tyler looked at Neil " Don't you like it " Neils stomach grumbled ahh Tyler thought hungry . " To be continued " Tyler got out first grabbing the towel one for Neil he.stepped out the shower .Grabbing the other towel drying himself .

" I'll go start breakfast " " Just toast " Tyler looked at Neil when he was drying. Neil stopped Tyler staring at him " What " " Not a big breakfast person " Neil shook his head never did since he was younger before school .

" Cereal then " Tyler asked Neil nodded then Tyler left to go start their breakfast leaving Neil to get dressed .

" WHAT ARE YOU DOING? Sam said, coming into the kitchen while Geraint was at the cooker. He looked around, " Going to make a sausage roll. " Sam tutted, shaking his head, coming over to Geraint. " Sam i'm able to make a sausage " Sam rolled his eyes he had only been out the hospital a week now and improving .But driving him nuts with certain things he was not supposed to be doing .

" IF YOU WANT A SAUSAGE " Sam took Geraint hand giggling, placing it at his crotch Geraint huffed " Maybe later " Geraint winked and gave Sam a peck on his nose . " i love you " " love you to now do you want one " .

" Go on then " Geraint watching Sam making the breakfast off sausages and eggs Geraint pinches Sam's bottom while he makes them bathe away until they are ready to eat Geraint makes the coffees it was so good to be out of the hospital and back to normality . Well normality ish.

1 MONTH IN, NEIL AND Tyler were inseparable. They stayed some nights at each other's flats. They were building up to go all the way. Neil wanted time to get to know Tyler even though they did other things. It was enough for now for the both them which was ok by Tyler

NEIL MET A COUPLE OF Tyler's friends who were nice and made him welcome which Neil was grateful for because Tuesdays thursday nights were tough after group therapy. Neil had been quiet after which Tyler let him be till he came round and the old nightmare Tyler would hold him till he felt better which Neil was grateful for and for Tyler being there for him . Neil had told him some things but not everything yet Tyler told him in his own time which was fine .

Janet and Roy were glad that Neil was happy and every lunch time like clock work Tyler came in for his lunch as usual and he was beginning to be part of the family Tyler also mentioned meeting his parents Neil had said not yet maybe wait a bit longer which Tyler agreed to .

Neil walked along the aisle of the supermarket collecting some groceries for himself. His phone beeped. Neil brought it out of his pocket. Tyler again told Neil that he and his friends were in Newcastle for Tyler's friend Oliver's bachelor weekend. The boys did ask Tyler to bring Neil but he declined because he wanted to let Tyler have a boys' weekend with his friends .

Tyler " did you remember to feed the boys " seriously Neil thought shaking his head

Neil " yes i remembered going over after shopping "

Tyler " i miss you ☺☹ "

Neil " Miss you to ❤ "

Neil turned the corner bumping into another Trolly jesus Neil thought looking up at Norman Petrie staring at him holy fuck Neil thought its been a while since he saw Norman " Neil " Norman smiled Neil nodded " Norman " .holy fuck I can't ignore him Neil thought since they have history and he has been good to me to .

Norman came over to Neil touching his arm " Neil where have you been i was worried " " i'm ok Norman im getting help and sober " Norman nodded and smiled looking him over " Neil we must catch up in fact if you have time now for a coffee " Shit Neil thought maybe I shouldn't brush him off but that would be bad Neil thought " Ok we can do that "

TYLER CHECKED HIS PHONE for the hundredth time which was annoying Al every time he went out to smoke what's he worrying about he thought even Oliver noticed to " Ty " he looked up at Al and back at his phone " Ty what's up " Tyler leaned against the railing he sighed thinking about Neil whether he is ok or not .

" Just Neil I worry about him " Al leaned against the railing beside Tyler he had told him about Neil and him going to therapy he was opening up more but it was taking time bit by bit Tyler not wanting to rush things . " Mate he will be fine you gotta stop worrying ok " " I know sorry " .Poor Tyler Al thought Neil was a nice person they were getting on well .

" Whose for an Indian " Alan, their other friend, comes out to see they all agreed to go for an Indian to soak up the alcohol. Oliver lay his arm around Tyler. He looked at him " ok now " Tyler nodded " Sorry just worry " .Oliver sighed he has been worried since they arrived he has just got to chill out he thought .

Norman insisted on paying for the drinks and muffins he talked constantly on how he had been what he was up to and how it wasn't the same with Neil not at Eden club he had met with a couple other people there was ok he said Norman did talk a lot whenever they had met previously. Maybe he should have other people, not just him, Neil thought while he listened .

" SOUNDS LIKE YOUR GOING to be busy Norman " " Oh o yes my work keeps me busy you know that Neil " Norman halved his muffin took a bite with some coffee " I have an exhibition coming up Neil would be good to see you there "

Neil sat forward drinking some of his coffee and muffin looked at Norman `` Thanks for the invite Norman " Neil looked at his phone he would have to get going soon he thought the fish would be fed soon . " Norman, I have to go. Norman touched Neil's arm before Neil stood up . " can I drop you off" " it's fine I can make my own way Norman " .

" SURE OK HAVE YOU ENOUGH to get back " " yes I do " Neil got up Norman stayed sitting Neil lifted his bags " please do keep in touch Neil " " will do Norman " Neil left Norman watched him go waved at Neil when he went outside he wondered what he had been up to all these weeks he thought .He looked well Norman thought which was good .

WHEN NEIL GOT TO TYLERS flat he got out the fish food he bent down looking at the fish while he sprinkled some food into the tank the three of them coming up to the top eating it Neil smiled he loved watching them eating and swimming around Tyler giggled every time Neil watched them . " Dad will be home soon boys " .

Neil thought about Norman Petrie god what will Tyler think whenever he tells him about him escorting he will try and explain that it was only for the money don't get yourself down about Neil thought . He got up and went into the kitchen taking out Tyler's food and putting them in the cupboard. He will come back later tonight so he can feed the boys in the morning before work .

WHEN HE GOT HOME HE left his bags in the kitchen and went to his secret hideaway to check stuff, opening the safe behind the picture in the bedroom, bringing out his old phone, putting it in the charger and opening up a bundle of notes. We're in the safe to take to the bank tomorrow. His old phone pinged beeped of messages and phone calls that would take him a while to get through he went into the safe again bringing out 3 usb sticks evidence he had around with him .Looking at them thinking i have to do this Neil thought i have got to be brave about it and not bottle it again .

To pluck up the courage to go to the police with there was an extra thousand sitting in the safe to incase he needed it and his bank cards he checked the time he had to go back to Tyler's flat check on the fish again after he has his shower first to check the messages from the old phone .

NEIL SPRINKLED THE fish food into the tank and as usual the fish came up the top taking the food while Neil watched them he bit his lip thinking about his plan he got up went into the kitchen sitting down at the desk to write a letter to Tyler pouring everything into the letter he had to know everything Neil thought and why tears running down his face Neil wiping them away .

After Neil chapped on Tylers neighbour a few minutes later Ellie answers the door her boyfriend behind her " Neil whats up " " Hi um .. can i leave Tylers key with you for the fish i got to go a family thing it's an emergency " is he ok she thought he looks upset .

Neil handed her the key and she looked at her boyfriend and back at Neil " of course are you ok i hope it's not serious' ' .

" hope not i'll let Tyler know " " ok Neil i'll check on the fish in the morning when is he back "

" Tomorrow and thanks "

Ellie shut the door she thought about Neil she was sure there was something else up " Hun " "yea " Ellie looked at her boyfriend looking concerned " what's wrong " " nothing let's get the rest the movie watched " Ellie looked round at the door she hoped it wasn't too serious with the family member .

NEIL WENT INTO THE police station going over to the desk the police man looked up at him " what can i do for you son "The police guy sighing looking up at Neil again " i'd like to speak to someone about a sensitive matter "

The police man sighed again isn't he bothered . Neil thought " Any complaints here is the website to go into " " uh it's not a complaint sir i want to report a crime " The police guy looked interested now Neil thought biting his lip time to get this sorted Neil thought .

NEIL SAT IN THE INTERVIEW room biting his nails. He had been there for at least ten minutes,how long are they gonna be? He thought . Then the door opened and Neil looked up at who it was . Officer Martin, who Neil knew from before, came inside . " Neil you ok you asked to speak to someone " Neil liked him he did listen to him about things before and could trust him .

" Yea i have evidence on something that you may want to know about " Neil brought out the usb sticks sliding them over to officer Martin to take Neil bites his lip " What's this" " Evidence you will need " .

AFTER THE POLICE STATION Neil went to the off licence and bought 2 bottles of vodka and then decided to make another purchase he went to the underpass where some of the homeless slept and where he sometimes slept whenever he didn't have anywhere to sleep at night .

Jan was walking along the road with a friend and noticed Neil coming out the off licence on the other side she was surprised had he gone back to his old ways she thought . " Jan " "Huh " she looked round as her friend looked over the street where Neil had disappeared. She had thought only she had stopped him to talk to him but she was off the clock . And could not interfere

"Jimmy" He looked round at Neil and was surprised to see him Jimmy put his hands in his hoodie " Neil where you been lately " " Around I "

" what you after "Jimmy asked looked round " ketamine , coke "

Jimmy went over to his bag looked up at Neil " cost you " " its fine i can pay " Jimmy brought out some pills and a bag coke handing it to Neil " looking at him is he having a party the amount he wants Jimmy thought

" I have ecstasy tablets for you planning a party " Jimmy asked Neil handing him his money " something like that thanks Jimmy " Neil gave a faint smile nodding, stuffing the pills into his rucksack .

" sure don't be a stranger now "

NEIL SAT PORTOBELLO beach tears running down his cheek drinking the bottle vodka it was burning his throat stupid stupid Neil thought no turning back now Tyler had been phoning constant 2 voice mails to the bottle vodka half drunk taking effect now .Neil looked up to the sky god forgive me for what I am about to do taking another slug of Vodka . It was starting to make him feel sick now but fuck it he thought taking more .

TYLER RAN INTO THE apartment shouting for Neil he looked in every room Al following behind him no Neil he looked over at the fish a note on the tank which areas Have been fed . The door chapped Al answered it Ellie Tyler's neighbour coming inside she looks over at Tyler looks at Al .

" Ellie " she looked between him and Al " Neil was here a couple hours ago. Something about a family matter gave me the key. Tyler looked at Al and back at Ellie. Could it be a family matter he thought was just a feeling he had that he couldn't shake he just wants Neil to be ok Tyler thought .

" Ty " Tyler looked round at Al in the kitchen holding up an envelope Tyler thanked Ellie and she left Tyler went into the kitchen taking the envelope from Al he opened it his hand shaking a two page letter to Tyler Neil pouring out everything that happened Tyler slumped on the chair tears sliding down his face From what he had read . " Ty talk to me " what the fuck is going on Al thought he sat beside Tyler he had his head in his hands . " What can I do? " Tyler looked up at Al. " We have to find him before he does something stupid " " ok we can do that .

Al got out his phone and what he was doing Tyler thought " What are you doing " " Calling for recruits " I guess we will need help to find Neil Tyler thought at least Al wants to help.

JAKE WAS TENDING BAR when the phone rang. Good job, it wasn't too busy . Tonight just a few regulars Julia was over at the other side taking orders. When he looked over she looked around and smiled when he went to answer the phone . " Hello Nero's " " Hi , Tyler is Darian by any chance' ' .

" sure he's here I'll patch you through "

Darian was at the filing cabinet when the phone rang he reached over to answer it just as Cameron came into the office " Hello " Boss it's Tyler on the phone " Jake patched him through Darian sat at his chair to take Tyler's call . "Tyler what can I do for you " " Darian it's Neil he's gone awol I'm really worried "

DARIAN LOOKS OVER AT Cameron and sits back on his chair " Tyler listen to me Malcolm was worried to that's why I have people out looking for him " That's good Tyler thought he looked up at Al who was also on the phone to people they knew to " That's good us to Darian I'm scared he's gonna do something I couldn't bear it " .

" I know I understand, just hang in there. I will update you. Oh, do you have a tracker on your phone? We are checking that out. " " I'll do that, thanks ."

Tyler thought that it was great that Malcolm was helping out as well as Darian please don't do anything stupid Tyler thought .

Chapter 20

Neil walked into Eden club looking around for the person he was looking for and spotted Sebastian up on the Vip holding court as usual Neil was feeling the effects off the bottle vodka he had drank but still had his bearings now one of Sebastian's security came over to him Neil looked at him " I want to talk to Sebastian " Neil asked his security went up to the vip while Neil waited .

SEBASTIANS SECURITY whispered in his ear he looked at him and nodded " Ladies , Gents can you please excuse us' ' They got up while Sebastian poured himself a whiskey he looked up at Neil standing at the door Sebastian smiled cocking his head smiling at Neil it's been a while he thought .

" It's good to see you Neil Come " Neil went nearer and stood facing him Sebastian patted the seat beside him Neil went over and sat beside him . " Where have you been Neil i was worried " yea right Neil thought i bet he wasn't grinning at Sebastian.

" Around i had time to think about stuff " Neil slurred Sebastian touched Neil's knee he cringed and smiled cringing inside Sebastian touching him " What was there to think about " " Just stuff Sebastian "

Seeing Neils face he smiled at him and then reached over to pour himself a whiskey and one for Sebastian. They clinked glasses and drank the contents of Neil watching Sebastian. Sebastian reached for the phone and ordered more drinks. Neil sat back listening to what he had ordered thinking i'm starting to get tired now Neil thought but i've got to think what i am doing .

" Sebastian " "Yes " Neil went nearer to him touching his knee looking at him " Lets go to the room ok " Sebastian smirked and nodded, reaching over for the phone again.Looking over at Neil smiling at him touching Sebastian's knee he grinned at Neil " Mmm fun is good " Sebastian exclaimed Neil smiled leaning into Sebastian " c'mon then " .

RAYMOND WISHED MARCUS would drive slower; he looked over at him and back at the road his phone pinged of a text he checked from Darian and Malcolm with updates Raymond looked at Marcus again ." Babe please drive slower " Marcus huffed yes there both anxious to get to Eden club but not speeding .Marcus shot his head hopefully nothing drastic will happen Marcus thought if Neil is drunk or high god knows what will happen .

Raymond put his hand on Marcus' knee he nodded looking at Raymond " Sorry " Raymond smiled and nodded to keep calm he thought his phone beeped of s text from Malcolm checking in again with his leads Raymond quickly texted him back they were just arriving at Eden club they would check in later with any update .

SEBASTIAN LAY HIS ARM round Neil in the private rooms his fangs descended Neil wiggled his finger at Sebastian " Now now Sebastian patience i have something for you " Sebastian licked his lips his fangs retracting again Sebastian grinned " You do " Neil went into his rucksack bringing out the vile he had made up for him looking round at Sebastian.

" What's that? " Neil held up the vial for Sebastian to see going nearer to him holding up the vile " something you might like Sebastian

I heard it's new on the street " Neil cocked his head biting his lip he looked interested Neil thought smiling again at Sebastian.

" Mmm really have you tried it looking at the Vile Sebastian's eyes gleaming with anticipation " Neil nodded and smiled Sebastian licked his lips again " Also ive heard its a mixture of donor blood not cheap though " . Sebastian hummed interestingly, then leaned over to take a drink . Neil noticing his bulge making him sick he looked at Sebastian again his eyes gleaming his long hair falling forward .

" i'd like to know who is the owner maybe i could work with him "

" I don't know that Sebastian I got it from a dealer I know I could always ask " Sebarian leaned forward going nearer to Neil touching his leg licking his lips vile man Neil thought to himself . " mmm ok find out " .

Doug looked up at the Vip no Sebastian where did he go he thought looking at his staff and back up at the Vip Thomas appeared what's worrying Doug he thought " Boss Sebastian is in the private rooms with Neil " Doug looked at Thomas what the hell he thought what's he doing in there with him . " Dougie " he looked at Thomad who handed him his phone. It was Darian calling him . What does he want now Doug thought getting involved in people's business Doug thought looking over at Thomas watching him .

" HAVE ANOTHER DRINK Sebastian " Neil handed him a glass of wine Neil smiled leaning his head on his hand on the couch Sebastian took a sip of his wine . Neil poured the vile in with Sebastian drink . "Bottoms up " Neil said watching Sebastian taking the drink of wine " What about you "Sebastian asked before he drank the wine " oh i only got it for you Seb "

Sebastian took all the drink Neil was watching on how long it would take effect " mmm interesting " " What Sebastian " Sebastian was slowly feeling the effects from the drug, a weird feeling he thought but I like it .

Neil watched Sebastian slowly get high with the effect of the ketamine he had given him the full dose just enough for his plan.neil went over to his rucksack looking over at Sebastian out of it good he thought he will be out for some time and the dosage he had given him would be enough to make him delirious .

Neil went over to Sebastian snapping his fingers ` ` Sebastian "He was totally spaced out when Neil checked him over his breathing laboured good Neil went into his pocket bringing out a syringe checking no it he then went to straddle Sebastian and was about to stick the syringe into Sebastian when a hand stopped him.

Neil looked round at Aida " Neil no " " DON'T STOP ME " Neil tried to get his hand back Aida squeezing harder Tears streaming down Neils face " Neil listen to me we have to get out of her now " .Neil was crying trying to get free of Aida I have to do this he thought .

" No i cant i don't care anymore i want to know what happened with Lainey "

Aida prized the syringe from Neil holding his arms ` ` Neil listen to me Tyler is waiting for you " fu Tyler Neil thought it's all a mess will he forgive him.he thought .

The door banged Aida looked round Marcus on the other side " Neil we have to go now the police are coming " The door opened Sebastian groaned everyone looked round at him " Aida lets go " Neil looked round at Marcus, Raymond and Aida .she took Neils hand and flitted off .

Marcus looked at Raymond and Sebastian " Babe " Marcus looked at Raymond he nodded and they ran off out the back to their car while Aida sped in hers with her driver Neil in the back crying Aida took his hand he pulled away huddled into himself he was so close . "Neil " "Leave me alone "

" Dougie what's going on " Thomas asked while the police piled into the club coming over to Doug handing him a search warrant Doug opened it up reading the contents he looked at Thomas `` Who is in charge here " Di Greenless appeared looking around the club people appearing from the back rooms wondering what's going on . " We are, " Doug said, looking at Thomas and back at Di Greenlees . " We need everything to check " " Of Course " .

Inga came rushing through going over to Doug whispering to him he looked at her " whose in charge here " An American voice from the back and more men appeared who the hell are they Doug and Thomas thought they were all built like footballers except for one which was a little smaller than the rest . " Di Greenless and who are you " " FBI " what do the FBI want to do with the business Doug thought showing their badges .

" This is our investigation " Gabriel announced looking at the others `` like hell it is who is your commanding officer " Gabriel looked at the others bringing out his phone while Seb brought out the paperwork for Di Greenless to check over . " Do I have to call my boss " " alright alright but i do need confirmation regarding this "

" Of course Gabriel said looking at the others while Seb dialled the no, handing it to Do Greenless ' ' Hello who is this " " Di Greenlees i am Julian the boss please cooperate with my men please' ' .

" right ok sure " Di Greenless handed back the phone to Seb Di Greenless shook his head " ok go on look for what you need " Di Greenless exclaimed exaggerated

Neil cried on Aidas shoulder in the car while she comforted him on the way back giving him words of comfort Oscar looked in the mirror at the two of them poor kid he thought he was in a right mess his phone beeped Raymond texting they were behind them the lights flashed he flashed his lights back .

" Why did you stop me i woulda done it " Aida swept Neils hair back comforting Neil he wiped his nose he leaned his head against the window poor kid she thought let him cry it out she thought .

DARIAN CAME INTO THE office where Tyler was standing. Please let it be good news " Neil is safe Aida has him there on their way back " Thank god Tyler thought of slumping back down onto the couch Malcolm came into the office he had let Janet and Roy know what was happening to since they have been calling constantly " Darian , Malcolm. Thank you " .

Malcolm. Looked at Darian and back at Tyler " no worries at least we found him "

ADELINE STOOD WATCHING Sebastian shaking her head while the policeman checked round the room she could smell something different from the wine glass he was definitely high on something she thought the police guy looked at Sebastian and at Adeline `` Whats. up with him is he high " " I expect so " Adeline sighed then someone came into the room she looked around at who it was and went over to Sebastian . Opening his eyes he could also smell something different " He's definitely high on something " Seb looked round at Adeline watching him .

" I'm guessing it'll wear off whatever he took " Seb said taking the glass putting into an evidence bag with the vile he looked up at the cctv that will need checked " it's Ketamine " Adeline explained Seb looked at her that's lethal stuff he thought " I didn't give him it " .Folding her arms sighing Seb looked around the room then Shane came in to help him looking over at Sebastian

" ADELINE " SHE LOOKED round at Ash coming into the room he looked at Seb who was over at Sebastian Ash got the cuffs out placing them on her " Do We need to take him to the hospital " Ash asked Seb shook his head looking at Ash " he just needs to sleep it off , " " yea looks like it " .

THE OFFICE DOOR OPENS Aida coming in with Neil Tyler stands god he's a mess Tyler thought tears streaming down Neils face he ran to Tyler both crying " shh I'm here your safe " " Ty I'm sorry " Tyler looks at the others mouthing thank you Darian leaves with Malcolm and Aida to let them talk Tyler and Neil sit on the couch Neil wipes his eyes .sniffing looking down at his hands afraid to look at Tyler .

" NEIL I " NEIL LOOKED down at his hands Tyler took his hands Neil looked up at him " I'll understand if you don't want to see me anymore I can take it " Tyler touched Neil's face also wiping his tears " you silly thing why would I do all. This to get you safe don't you get it Neil I'm falling for you "

What the hell Neil thought after what he had said in the letter and him nearly killing Sebastian Neil leaned into Tyler crying Tyler comforting him " Neil we need to get you home a bath and sober up ok we can talk about stuff in the morning " Neil looked up at Tyler and nodded wiping his nose . " I would've done it, you know I wouldn't have cared if he died ' .

" shhhh don't think like that please Neil " " I mean it Tyler fuck why are you so calm about this " Neil got up pacing the room Tyler watching him " Neil sit down let's be calm about this " .Tyler reaching for him Neil pulling away " I could have helped her Ty but " Neil paced again Tyler watching him he has to get him home Tyler thought he needs sleep .

" YOU BEING TO FUCKING nice to me Tyler it's suffocating it's happened to me my uncle " Neil started crying again Tyler went to him holding him Neil punching at his chest " Neil you need sleep " Neil looked up at Tyler moving away from him " I need another drink and a hit I can't do it Tyler I've tried but the voices in my head are telling me to " .

Fuck Tyler thought what to do in this situation. " I'll go to a meeting " Neil said Tyler went to him hugging Neil again the door chapped Janet and Roy walks into the office Neil goes to them all three hugging Janet and Roy reassure Tyler watching I want to understand him . Like Alec they couldn't help him either but this time Tyler was determined to get Neil clean and sober.Then Malcolm comes in and stands at the door Cameron behind him he looks at Cameron they head back up to the bar best to leave them to tal Malcolm thought .

Marcus and Raymond arrive back at the club to the bar where Darian and the others are, they look over at the Council enforcers over at the far side drinking and talking . " where. Marcus asks " There in the office talking " Malcolm says sighing Marcus and Raymond hoped Neil was ok Raymond looked at Marcus leaning into him it's been exhausting running around looking for Neil .

" How much have they had? " Malcolm asks Darian, looking over at the Council enforcers. " There on their third round of shots, " Darian says, then his phone rings a facetime call from Julian . He excused himself connecting the call " Darian how are you and are they behaving "

Darian giggled looking over at the boys " Yes Julian they are fine " Darian turned the phone round for Julian to see and turned it back " Good and for Sebastian he will be ok going to take him a while to get round " .

That's good Darian thought a relief for Neil maybe " The CCTV we have sorted and also we need to chat to Neil whenever he feels up to it " " will let him know ".

" Thank you as for Lainey we are on the lookout " That's good Darian thought Neil needs closure from that for him to move on after his call from Julian Darian went back over to the bar it has been an exhausting day he out his arm round Malcolm kissed his head Malcolm looked up at Darian and smiled leaning into him .

" YOU KNOW THIS PLACE isn't to bad " Gabriel said pouring himself another whiskey and it's good stuff he thought these Scots know how to make good drinks " Not bad " Seb said smirking Shane looked round at Darian and back at Seb he kicked him under the table " what was that for " " you are married man now and he's married to his partners " Seb huffed Ashlyn shook his head . " This is your type place Seb " Seb glared at Gabriel who giggled .

" Shut up " Seb said shaking his head he can still look and look he did shaking his head again " Text from Julian " Shane said everyone checking the group chat text " Gentlemen is there anything else I can get you " They all looked up at Darian with Cameron beside him " Thanks Darian were good we're heading off soon and thanks for the hospitality " the guys looked at Seb why the hell is he being so polite all of a sudden . " you are welcome and any news regarding Lainey " . Darian asked, looking between the guys .

" OUR PEOPLE ARE STILL searching. We should get a new one soon. "" Good, " Darian and Cameron were about to leave when Shane asked Cameron about the books " Thank you in the middle of writing no 3 at the moment " .So kind of him to ask Cameron what pleased him Darian smiling at him .

" My wife Marina loves your work " Gabriel confessed he looked at the guys and back at Cameron he smiled " She would be mad if I didn't get your autograph " Cameron looked at Darian and back at them . " I will personally send them myself and can do one better by taking a selfie with you guys" The Guys whopped what a nice guy they all thought and a lucky guy being with Darian too .

Gabriel brought out his phone juggling on the right pose to take Malcolm watching them honestly what are they doing his phone beeped Sam texting asking about updates Malcolm texting him back what has happened about Nei

he would update him soon there was still to find out about Neil's friend Lainey . Malcolm heard giggling from the table with the council Enforcers chatting away Darian looked over at Malcolm Cameron and looked round so he laid out his hand for Malcolm to come to them .

" This is Malcolm " Cameron explained everyone said hello " Question " Seb asked Shane kicked him he glared at Malcolm. Sniggered " If you're wondering about the three of us Seb " Malcolm asked shit my big mouth he thought " No it's great isn't it guys " Who all agreed but Seb was curious to know about the sleeping arrangements even though he had a few threesomes in the past .

NEIL FELL ASLEEP ON Tyler's shoulder on the way back to his flat Roy drove them back Neil poured his heart out how he was feeling and he had thought about going into residential therapy which Tyler thought was a good idea instead of going to twice weekly therapy he would definitely try to help him through it .

JANET CAME UP TO THE flat with them incase Tyler needed help with Neil Tyler had his arm round Neil's shoulder before he took him to the bedroom Neil turned round to Janet " Janet thanks for everything " Janet nodded tears stung her eyes thinking about her son then they went into the bedroom she hoped Neil would get better .She and Roy couldn't help there son but they would help Neil whenever he needed her .

NEIL SAT N THE BED while Tyler got him pjs out to wear while Neil started Striping god he was dog tired and needed sleep " You wanna go for a shower " Neil shook his head got into the pjs and crawled into bed Tyler sat beside him smoothing his hair back and bending to kiss his cheek then getting up looked round at him before leaving . He kept the door ajar incase Neil needed him. Tyler leaned against the door and shut his eyes. Please give me strength to get through this Tyler though .

Janet was sitting on the couch when Tyler came through "Hes sleeping " Tyler went into his cupboard to get a couple blankets out " Tyler it's a lot to deal with you know " Tyler knew that but he was prepared to do it .he loves Neil thats for sure and his experience with his friend Alec .

" Janet i can handle it i have experience in this our friend Alec it's been three years since he passed " " im so sorry to hear that Tyler "

Tyler sat at the kitchen table Janet watching him he looked up at Janet " We all tried with him but Alec wasn't for saving he overdosed " " i'm so sorry to hear that " Tyler nodded he got back up " Thanks for your help "

Janet left Tyler checked on Neil. He was sleeping well. He thought he needed it. He left a glass of water on the side table leaving the room going into the lounge sorting the covers and laying on the couch . His Phone beeped of a text Oliver texting checking in Tyler texted him back letting him know what's happened and will catch up soon . Tyler tried to sleep, his mind racing; it took him.a while to eventually fall asleep .

NEIL KICKED HIS LEGS, his throat closing, finding it hard to breathe so dark. Why is it so dark burning? He felt burning and screamed sitting up in bed looking around Tyler coming rushing in . Neil was disoriented, where Tyler is looking at him .

" Tyler " " I'm here " They hugged thirsty Neil though Tyler looked at him touching Neils face " Where did you go " " Slept on the couch "
.

" Why " " To let you sleep " Tyler stood up went round the other side getting into bed sliding his arm round Neil he heard his phone beep ignoring it Tyler kissed Neils head . " I was scared " " You want to talk about it " .

" not really Tyler don't go " " I'm here go to sleep "

AFTER FIVE MINUTES Tylet heard Neil's light snoring good he thought he would need it snuggled into each other until Tyler fell asleep again .

THOMAS HELD DOUG'S hand in the interview room at the police station. They let him in for five minutes. Thomas had been crying.

Doug could tell " Baby don't cry " " it's bad Dougie what are we gonna do " .

Indeed Doug thought what are they going to do " The things they have said Dougie " Doug sighed he sat back scrubbing his face yes some things he.did and didn't know about Eden club since it was Adeline that owned it .

" Thomas listen to me when i get out we will start somewhere else ok " Thomas nodded wiping his.eyes " Marbella like wd talk about " Doug nodded it's the best solution they thought no more these clubs maybe going to Marbella would be better for Thomas with his condition for His Hunting's and with the heat it would be better for his condition.

THE DOOR OPENED ONE the police mem coming inside with notes looking up at Doug and Thomas " your lawyer is here " They looked at each other Lawyer Doug thought I didn't plan to get a lawyer he thought . " Hello I'm Ford Allan " Thomas and Doug look up at him standing at the door he seemed older they both thought with sprinklings of pepper hair he sat down taking out his notepad and looked up fixing his glasses .

" Darian sent me " wow Thomas thought that's generous of him sending him a lawyer to deal with his problem the door chapped the door opens again Seb coming into the room to oh wow Doug though he is tall and very muscular they both thought . " I'm Seb " .

Chapter 21

Doug and Thomas walked through the airport in Edinburgh to get their flight to Marbella; they couldn't believe it when they were released from the police station and the Council Enforcer and Darians Lawyer helped out; they were free to go and set up a new life in Spain which they both had talked about .

Doug checked the flight times Thomas stood Doug looked round at him smiling " ok " Thomas nodded going over to Doug `` Perfect I can't wait for Spain " Doug smiled he was to a new life for both of them . " c'mon let's get checked in " Doug lay his arm round Thomas' arm leading the way to the check in desk to their new life in Spain together .

TYLER TURNED TO THE side, laying out his hand to snuggle into Neil, his side empty. Tyler sat up checking the time just after 8 in the morning where Neil Tyler thought about getting up going through to the lounge . Tyler saw Neil at the fish tank watching the fish in the thank god Tyler thought Neil smiled and looked up at him Tyler coming over to Neil sitting beside him looking at him Tyler lay his arm round Neil .

" I just fed them. " Thanks. " They look at each other. He looks tired Tyler thought how long has he been up for" Tyler." " Mmm" Neil took Tyler's hand. They looked at each other again. " I'm ok " Tyler nods and gives a faint smile as he goes to get up . "Breakfast " " Sure i'll help " .

Neil gets up to follow Tyler into the kitchen " Ty " he looks round at Neil " i've called the rehab place " Tyler went over to Neil hugging him that's a good step he thought Neil slid his arms round Tyler's waist then Tyler looked at him touching Neil's face . " You've made the right choice " It was Malcolm that suggested that he had texted a couple places to check out there, " gonna get back to me " .

" good now what you hungry for " Tyler went to move Neil stopped him Tyler looked at Neil ` ` what is it " "About what I said last night and in the letter don't you want to talk about it " Tyler sighed leaned against the counter taking Neil's hand " Neil let's not today ok I've taken today off to look after you let's just have a normal day ok " Neil nodded Tyler went over to the fridge bringing out the milk butter and jam . Neil got the bread while Tyler got the cereal, pouring some in each bowl. Neil's phone rang checking the caller ID. He didn't know the no but connected the call anyway .

" Hello " " Neil it's Seb from the Council " Neil looked over at Tyler who looked round at Neil going into the lounge " Any news " " Yes can we arrange to come over to you " " Sure I'm at Tyler's I'll text you the address " After the call Neil went back into the kitchen letting Tyler know about Seb coming over . Neil had a thumping headache from the vodka but taking a painkiller wouldn't be a good idea he would ride it through and a shower would help too . Neil yawned. He was still tired. Tyler noticed while preparing the breakfast that Neil looked over at Tyler. He was so good to him he thought last night must've freaked him out and he still wants to be with me. Neil couldn't believe it .

AFTER AN HOUR SEB ARRIVED with one other person Shane my god he and Tyler thought they were very tall and muscular, not as much as Shane who was a bit smaller in size it was just all a blur last night Seb handed Neil an envelope with information. He would need to look at he looked exhausted, Seb thought . Neil looked at the envelope he was dreading opening it . " Just so you know Eden club had been shut down and Sebastian locked up very securely as for him and Adeline they will be put on trial " Shane explained Tyler looked at Neil and back at Seb and Shane .

" Here " Tyler asked, looking between the three of them Neil took Tyler's hand looking at Seb and Shane " no Ty there own council court " what does he mean Tyler thought looking at Seb and Shane and back at Neil then it hit him no way they don't exist nor do they he thought . " Holy fuck " Neil sniggered Shane at Seb rules were they were not allowed to reveal themselves . " Julian is dealing with things back home till we have finished our findings here, " Seb explained .

Neil picked up the envelope, opened it, taking out the piece of paper information about Lainey, her death and where she was found. Neil always knew she wasn't alive; he had that feeling in his gut . " in a way I know that she isn't suffering anymore " " Her family has been contacted " That's good Neil thought it still hurt that he won't see her anymore but he will have memories of Lainey . Looking after each other on the streets sometimes she would stay with friends for a couple nights or meet up with someone but Neil did insist she keep Neil informed that she was ok and him her the same .

AFTER SEB AND SHANE left Tyler tidied up while Neil wanted to change then realised he had no spare clothes with him he went into the kitchen Ftler at the sink his head bowed his shoulders shaking Neil went to him holding Tyler he turned to Neil sliding his arms around his waist . " i don't want to break up " what the hell Neil thought, what made him feel like that Neil thought .

" Ty what's got into you " Tyler looked at Neil wiping his eyes " I just thought with you wanting to go to rehab you wanted to work on yourself " Neil snorted shaking his head " Ty i don't want to break up with you silly " Tyler looked up at Neil shocked at what he said but in his letter he said he wanted him to have a good life whoever he ended up with .

" But your letter is " Neil touched Tyler's face wrapping his arm around his neck " Tyler i wasn't in the right headspace " Tyler moved away from Neil slumped on the kitchen table he was so exhausted by all this . " I love you " Tyler said looking up at Neil oh wow he said it first Neil thought . Neil smiled leaning against the sink, Neil staring at Tyler .

" you don't have to say it back just yet when you're ready to " Neil moved to Tyler sitting beside him they looked at each other Neil smiled taking Tyler's hand . " My boyfriend is declaring his love first " Tyler's eyes widened and they moved closer to each other bumping heads . " I love you too. Tyler wrapped his arms around Neil and they kissed . Wow Tyler thought there was somewhere Tyler touching Neil's face he leaned into his touch .

" Shall we celebrate " Tyler asked cocking his head smirking " Can we wait when i get out from rehab but we could do something else " They kissed Neils phone rang should i leave it call back best not Neil answers the phone it was the rehab place offered him a place starting tomorrow that was quick he thought the sooner the better he thought and Tyler thought so to .

AFTER THE PHONE CALL Tyler took Neils hand leading him to the bathroom both getting into the shower Tyler pinning Neil to the tile kissing him Neil wrapped his arms round Tyler's shoulders there cocks hard grinding into each other " Ty " " mmmm " Tyler kissed licked Neil's neck " I am clean you know my last test was 3 months ago " Tyler looked at Neil touching his face he nodded kissed Neil's nose . " Same but I do like to be careful " . Neil nodded, smiling at Tyler moving closer to him. They kissed again. Neil moaned .

" Me to " Tyler moved his hand down to Neil's cock stroking him he closed his eyes while Tyler wanked him off Neil whimpered there were other things he wanted to talk to Tyler about to Tyler looked at him where did he go Tyler thought he looked deep in thought . " Neil " " I'm ok just thinking " Tyler snorted thinking what he was thinking about Neil .

TYLER GOT THE SHAMPOO. Neil wet his hair and let Tyler wash his hair. It felt so good someone else did it for you. Ty there's other stuff a wanna tell you " " Rinse " Neil rinsed his hair sticking his head under the water . Neil turned his head Tyler at the back of him " One step at a time ok " Neil nodded Tyler kissed his cheek " Now let's get you dried and bed " . Neil smirked, Tyler slapped his bottom, Neil yelping . " Not that " Neil pouted then got out both drying themselves " What I mean was to rest more I'll go to your flat and get what you need sound ok "

Neil nodded Tyler handing him his pjs more sleep sounded good Neil thought hopefully he would getting into his pjs going into the bedroom getting under the covers while Tyler got ready " Ty will you change the code " " I will what else " " bring whatever is in the safe leave it here for you to look after and obviously clothes " Tyler snorted going over to Neil sitting beside him .

Tyler bent to kiss Neil again touching his face "I won't be long o " Neil nodded Tylsr got up and looked round before leaving Neil curled into the covers Tyler smiled then shut the door just keep your cool Tyler he thought we will get through this he and his friends will help him get through it .

, ********

Tyler looked around Neils flat. There was a half bottle of vodka sitting on the lounge table Tyler picked it up taking it to the kitchen pouring the contents down the sink then putting the bottle in the bin tidied up a bit then went to the picture punching in the no there was money and his bank cards another usb stick another vile of something not touching that Tyler thought he shut the safe punching in a new no.

He was about to leave when the door chapped Tyler went to open it to Roy standing there " Roy come in I'm just getting some things for Neil " " good Janet's been frantic we called earlier no answer "

" sleeping he's exhausted " " Good he will need it " Tyler folded the clothes into the rucksack Roy watched Neil go into the bedroom a mess he thought he would have to sort that soon coming back into the lounge Roy on the phone he could guess Janet had called him .

" Just updating Janet " "The rehab place called he goes in tomorrow " Roy nodded that's good he thought it what he needs time away get himself clean and sober Tyler looked up at Roy there's something he wants to ask he thought " Roy just say it " Roy looked over at Tyler he sat on the couch beside Roy " Oh I well It's Janet really she just worries you see and it's a big thing to take on you know " .

" Roy I have experience in that my friend Alec he died of an overdose three years ago " " oh I'm sorry to hear that it's just well " Tyler stood up taking the rucksack into the kitchen and coming back into the lounge " you don't have to worry Roy I can handle it " Roy nodded he hoped so and he can rely on him and Janet to if needed .

" I love him Roy and I would do anything for Neil when he needs me " Well that's certainly a good boyfriend Roy thought he stood up patting Tyler on the shoulder " You certainly have guts Tyler "

I sure do, he thought and I've been through it with Alec and this time Neil will survive this no matter how long it takes him Tyler will support him all the way .

NEIL WAS HAVING A NICE dream of Lainey. She was in a field walking through sunflowers. She was bright and happy. She was with other people running and laughing along the sunflower field . Lainey stood at the door, she looked over at Lucien and back at Neil asleep in the bed "Are you giving him a happy dream aren't you " Lucien looked at Lainey and nodded, " That's good she thought .

Lainey went over to the bed while Lucien watched her bending down facing Neil she whispered to him " You don't have to worry anymore I'm happy now " Lainey looked round at Lucien he nodded again a bright light caught Laineys attention looking round she had a sense of peace come over her . Lucien came nearer to Lainey. She looked up at him and he held out his hand Lucien nodded towards the light .Lainey looked back one more time before disappearing into the light .

Lainey stood up taking Lucien's hand they walked towards the light she looked round at Neil one more time before she disappeared into the light holding Lucien's hand Neil woke up suddenly " LAINEY " He looked round he was dreaming and lay back down rubbing his head was her telling him she was at peace . Neil sat up again looking at his phone the time after two was it only an hour he was asleep felt like hours and lay back down . He had two missed calls, two texts from Darian and Malcolm; he will text them back later and one was from the rehab place.

Tyler got back to his Flat finding Neil in the kitchen making food Tyler shook his head he should be in bed he thought going into the kitchen Neil looked round and Smiled " How long have you been up " Tyler sat Neils rucksack on the table " Not long " Neil went over to his rucksack Tyler looked over at the counter Neil had made sandwiches Tyler thought that's progress he must be feeling better .

" I thought you would have slept longer. " Neil looked up at Tyler while going through his bag. " Rehab called again making sure I still wanted the place. " Tyler thought maybe I should have brought the whole lot and Neil could move in whenever he was ready .

Neil bringing out his clothes looking up at Tyler watching him " Ty what is it " " um i think so apart from a vile of something you had in the safe " shit Neil thought he had forgot that was in there . " what's in it Neil ". Neil looks at Tyler biting his lip looking into the rucksack again .

" I forgot I had it, did you get rid of it? " " No, I wasn't sure what it was. Tyler went to Neil, turning him to face him. " You must be honest with each other, Neil . " Neil looked away, tears stinging his eyes . " Don't baby me Tyler I'm done with the stuff please believe me " Tyler hugged Neil he wrapped his arms round Tyler holding him tight shutting his eyes . I am definitely done with the drugs and alcohol now Neil thought and I want to be with this man too .

" Good " Tyler moved away from Neil he went over to the kettle, filling it. Neil went into the bedroom to get changed. Tyler , thinking about Roys words, leaned against the counter while the kettle was boiling.im not giving up on him Neil came back through dressed in his joggers and hoodie .

" what time did the rehab place say you have to be there for " " Afternoonish " Tyler started to make the drinks Neil went into his bag bringing out his wallet going into it and there was a picture of him and Lainey when they took it at one the photo booths .Neil touched the photo smiling about that time Tyler turned to ask Neil something seeing him looking at his wallet he went to him hugging Neil a sob came out of him Tyler gave him words of comfort.

" I had a dream about her. She was happy running in a field of sunflowers. " Tyler smoothed Neils hair back. He was starting to open up a bit more now. " Maybe that was her way of telling you she was ok. " Tyler kissed Neils temple and he closed his eyes . " Neil were you and Lainey " Neil snorted and looked at Tyler " Definitely not we looked out for each other " " That's good " .Neil cocked his head wrapping his arms around Tyler then his stomach grumbled. He is hungry after all Neil thought even though he wasn't earlier .

" Let's eat " Tyler took Neil's hand guiding him over to the table then Tyler went to make the drinks while Neil checked his bag bringing out his bank cards and money " Ty will you keep these for me " Neil sat them on the table Tyler turned round bringing over the drinks " " Sure anything for you "

" I was thinking about getting a tattoo " whatever for Tyler thought Neil sliding up his sleeve exposing his scar on his wrist Tyler took his hand Neil looked at him Tyler lifting up his arm kissing his wrist Neil stopped breathing for a second tearing staring at Tyler . " Good idea what kind " " Not sure yet " . That was tough for Neil exposing his scar to Tyler at that point he felt brave but vulnerable. It was good that Tyler was understanding him more than Neil thought .

NORMAN PETRIE CHAPPED on Darians office door biting his lip a few seconds later the door opened by Darian Jake came out of the office nodded at Norman Darian appeared what's up he wondered Norman looking worried he thought " Norman come in " Norman stepped into the office Darian went over to the desk sitting at his chair Norman sat on the other side .

" what can I do for you Norman " " i was wondering how Neil was "

Darian sat back in his chair well someone who actually cares how Neil is he thought Darian sat forward in his chair leaning his arms on the desk " He is doing ok it will take him a while to get back to himself he will be going into Rehab"

Norman was startled hearing the news but if it's what he needs that be good he thought " Good good " " you don't have to worry Norman Tyler is looking after him "

Who is Tyler Norman thought Neil didn't mention him before Darian got up coming round to Norman's side leaning against his desk

" Tyler is Neil's boyfriend it's just recent but by the sounds of it just what Neil needs Norman "

Norman looks up at Darian he's right Someone his own age Norman gets up straightens his jacket " Good to know Thank you I'm pleased that he is getting the help he needs "

TYLER AND NEIL LAY in bed Neils head on Tylers chest holding hands Tyler kissed Neils head " I didn't sleep with all of them " Neil looked up at Tyler`` Neil you don't need " Neil sat up pulling the sheet up round his waist he bit his lip Tyler looking at him this is it I'm going to tell him everything now Neil thought .

" i want to Ty i only did it for the money to try and get a place my own get away from that dingy bed sit also wanting to get clean and Sober to it was hard Ty "

Tyler crossed his legs he touched Neils face he leaned into Tyler's his touch " some of them just wanted company to talk like Norman Petrie he's lonely Ty his partner died three years ago they were together for years' ' .

" That's sad "Tyler said it must have been hard for the man to deal with his partner's death Neil thought so too even though they had.sex a couple times Norman had to use viagra to perform.. Most times but the man was just lonely most the time they had met up he was the nicest out of them too .

" I want to do something for Janet and Roy " Neil got up but naked went into his rucksack bringing out the thousand pounds he had looking over at Tyler watching him " I want to give them money for the cafe " " That's a lot Neil " . Jesus it was a lot Tyler thought and very generous amount to he hoped they would be grateful for it .

Neil went back over to bed, getting in, Tyler lay his arms round him " i know but they have been so kind to me " " ok fine I guess it'll be a start for them " Neil nodded looking up at Tyler Neil hoped that Janet and Roy would be ok about it .

TYLER KISSED NEIL THEY lay down facing each other its was late they should try get some sleep Tyler touched Neil's face and kissed his temple he's been brave telling him half his past he knew Neil wanted to tell him more he just needs time to Neil moved closer to Tyler he kissed him he kissed his chin his cheek his neck moving down licking his nipple . Tyler arched groaning while Neil licked and sucked at his nipple Neil looked up grinning Tyler flushed Neil moving down stroking Tyler licking At his cock Tyler groaned again Neil took him in his mouth sucking Tyler lifted one leg giving Neil more aces .

Neil squirted some lube onto his finger bending down again sucking and flicking a finger in and out of Tyler's entrance Tyler gripped the sheet he was gonna come soon Neil moved up kissing Tyler still stroking him Neil went down to take him in his mouth again so good Tyler thought gripping the sheet again .That is so good Tyler thought Neil licking sucking on his nipple Tyler groaned .

Tyler came on a shout Neil came after they both lay facing each other when Neil got out from Rehab they will take it to the next level " I love you " Tyler said first kissed Neil " Love you to " Eventually they fell asleep after their third make out session both exhausted by it .

Chapter 22

N eil looked up at the building when he came out the car he looked over at Tyler coming round to his side giving him his rucksack when they got to the door a lady came out to greet them introducing herself Helen her name was they both went inside didn't look to bad Neil thought looking at Tyler while Helen took them round the facilities and giving Neil a leaflet on the rehab centre .Helen telling them about the facilities and when it opened .

" Dr Armstrong will be here soon. You will be up on the second floor Neil "" ok and visiting " Neil looked at Tyler and back at Helen she looked between Neil and Tyler .Neil hoped the others would visit him if they could .

" We advise residents to have visitors once or twice a week depending on their stay. You can discuss that later there is paperwork to attend to first " Helen looked between them again Neil and Tyler nodded listening to what Helen had to say , maybe should leave them to it so he can get settled in and let them have some private time before Tyler leaves .

AFTER THE PAPERWORK was done Helen took him to his room not too bad , more like a hotel he thought residents were encouraged to all eat together which was fine. He and Tyler arranged for him to visit at the end of the week to let him get settled and that he agreed with Helen he would stay for two months . And if after the two months Neil didn't think he was ready to go home he would stay another month Tyler thought two months would be enough for Neil. And for Neil to .

THOMAS STOOD OUT ON the veranda of there Marbella home looking out to the sea arms wrapped around his waist Doug kissing his neck Thomas turned his head to face Doug he smiled " alright " " mmmm " coming to Marbella helped with Thomas condition different weather from the uk and even the doctors at the local hospital said the same it would be much better for Thomas and less stress to . Definitely less stress and for Doug to Thomas thought and the apartment was just perfect the steps were not too bad for Thomas and it was a reasonable size villa for them .

Which was not far from the arena, the bar's shops which Doug thought would be perfect for Thomas if he couldn't manage to walk far they did discuss getting a mobility scooter for Thomas which they would find out about soon since his condition was getting worse with his Huntingdons .

" YOU WERE SO RIGHT Dougie suggesting we move here " yes indeed Doug thought he took a sip his wine leaning against the railing Thomas looked at him " So what do you think of the wine bar then " There it is Thomas thought they hadn't even thought about that since moving " let's think about it first ok " Definitely think about it Thomas thought he didn't wasn't anything to stressful .

" Ok " Doug kissed Thomas he knew he would ask about that sometime but for now Thomas just wanted me time and couples time for now to settle into their new home Doug lay his arm round Thomas looking out to the Bay Area sipping his wine . Thomas lay his head on Dougs shoulder " Lets not leave Doug " .

He is so right Doug thought why would we leave this is our dream to live abroad since they were in their two year anniversary also and the benefits of a better life in Spain to especially for Thomas with his Condition .

Epilogue

2 Months Later

Geraint looked between Dr Morris and Sam did he hear him right his cancer was gone he was now in Remission Tears ran down Sam's face he couldn't believe it all these months of Chemo hospital appointments his husband was now cancer free . " I don't know what to say Dr Morris but thank you we can start our lives again " Dr Morris smiled he was pleased about Geraint progress and he was Cancer free .

Geraint looked at Sam taking his hand we can get back to normal now he thought " i will schedule your 6 months check up Geraint it's necessary but if you feel you need sooner just make an appointment "

" I will be Dr Morris and Thanks again Sam and I can get on with our lives now right babe " Sam nodded and smiled definitely Sam thought no more hospital appointments from now on start making baby arrangements soon too .

They came out the hospital Geraint looked up at the sky Sam watching him Geraint looked over at him laying out his hand Sam took out " Let's make a baby " Sam snorted shaking his head " Club first " they walked to the car got in Geraint reaching over to Sam " i cant wait till we get home "

Geraint kissed Sam "Babe calm down " they both giggled Geraint taking Sam's hand placing it on his crotch oh wow Sam thought blushing he looked at Geraint. " We won't stay long, ok ? " Geraint nodded. Sam started the car driving off to the club, grinning .

" Ah Man that's great guys' ' Malcolm was pleased about Geraint's news he was cancer free Darian came round from the table shaking Geraint's hand " Champagne ' ' Sam looked at Geraint Malcolm looked between them what's going on with those two he thought .Are they not happy with the news Malcolm thought .

" Thanks Darian but I have my parents to see right Sam " " That's right we did promise didn't we " .Sam smiled at Geraint looking round at the others who all had a puzzled look on their faces Malcolm smirked he knew exactly what they were gonna be up to .

MALCOLM SNORTED, SHAKING his head, yeah right he thought they two were gonna have sex Darian wondered what was going on Geraint and Sam were about to leave when Cameron arrived with Philip who was 6 months now . Darian took him from Cameron taking him to the table Sam and Geraint looked at him. He was such a good father just like they will someday .

" Geraint is cancer free " Malcolm announced that's great news Cameron thought while they both walked to the door saying their goodbyes where are they going Cameron thought . " Are they in a hurry for something? " Malcolm lay his arm around Cameron. He looked down at him. He winked at Cameron. Ahh, he thought they were going to have sex with them, Cameron thought .

NEIL PACKED THE REST of his clothes two months had passed so quickly the rehab had helped, talking to Dr Armstrong one on one twice weekly helped and seeing Tyler twice weekly helped too and Janet and Roy came to visit once a week bringing news of home and the Coffee shop . They thanked him for the money and told him of their plans for the coffee shop to extend it and some Diy to the coffee shop which pleased Neil they deserved it he thought since they had been good with him they met .

Neil also made a couple friends one had gone home the other had a couple weeks to go the door chapped Neil looked round at Bob one the rehab volunteers " Tylers here " " Thanks " Bob came into the room Neil looked around the room in case he forgot anything and felt nervous about going home .

" Neil " he looked round at Bob picking up his bag " i just can't believe it went so quick " They walked out his room to the landing and Bob patted his back . " You have done good Neil, you know what to do when you feel overwhelmed " " i do thanks Bob "

Tyler waited at reception for Neil. He was nervous and excited that Neil was coming home today. Everyone else was excited to see him too . The door opened and Neil walked out with one of the volunteers. Neil smiled and ran to Tyler ." Hi " " Hi " .Hugging each other. I am so happy to be going home now, Neil thought .

They got into the car Tyler looked round at Neil he looked refreshed and happy which was good he thought Tyler took his hand Neil looked at him " Ty I'm ok " " Good cause everyone is excited to see you " shit Neil thought everyone is great but I just want to be with Tyler right now Neil thought while Tyler drove along the road . " Ty " . " mmm " Tylsr looked round at Neil taking his hand again " To be honest I'm feeling a Little overwhelmed can we just go to your place "

" Babe it's fine course we can Janet will understand " I feel bad for saying it now " Neil bit his lip Tyler took his hand squeezing it .

He shouldn't feel bad Tyler thought besides it's a big thing coming out of Rehab for him Tyler lifted Neil's hand kissing it Neil smiled he reached over to Tyler " Besides we have a lot catching up to do right " Tyler smirked Neil laying his hand on Tyler's knee careful he thought don't wanna crash the car Neil kissed the side of Tyler's cheek . Tyler was hard and shifted in the car seat noticed by Neil who smirked .

PHOEBE LOOKED OUT THE window at the coffee shop and checked her watch for the hundredth time. What's keeping them? Tyler went to pick up Neil ages ago Darren sighed for the hundredth time Phoebe glared at him shaking her head .

" Guys Tyler just called, they have decided to just go to Tylers Neil will see everyone soon " Janet said looking at Roy he nodded " is he ok " ,Phoebe asked coming over to Janet " Yes he's fine c'mon let's pack up " .

Phoebe looked up at the welcome home bunting Janet looked at her " Let's leave it up ok " . Good idea Phoebe thought because I'm not putting it back up again .Phoebe sighing while packing things away

TYLER AND NEIL PUSHED through the door kissing Tyler pushed Neil against the wall dropping the bags Tyler grinded against Neil he whimpered Tyler kissing his neck . The lights of the fish tank illuminating Neil looks round at the fish smiling as he misses the little guys. Noticing them swimming around .

" Ty let me say hello to the boys' ' Tyler looked at Neil then looked over at the fish Tyler took Neil's hand leading him to the tank they bent down in front of the tank Neil thought Angel looked fatter than before or was he imagining it inspecting the tank at a different angle .

" Tyler Angel " Neil pointing to the fish Tyler grinned " Well it turns out Angel is not a he but a she and one those two got her pregnant " " No way " Tyler nodded wow Neil thought that's a revelation . " How many do you think? " " vets say it might be multiple " .Oh Wow Neil thought that's amazing inspecting the fish again.

Neil moved closer to Tyler wrapping his arms around his shoulders kissing him " Now where were we " Tyler smiled they kissed again Tyler moving Neil to the floor kissing him " Ty the kids " Tyler snorted they bumped heads seriously he thought it's not as if they can see properly they are fish afterwall And I have been away from my love for to long Tyler thought .

Tyler stood up held out his hand Neil stood up they kissed again Tyler slid his hand round Neils waist leading him to the bedroom. Tyler went over to the drawer to get the condoms and lube Neil watched biting his lip Tyler came over to Neil they kissed Neil taking off Tyler t-shirt Tyler doing the same with Neils while they kissed .

" I'm nervous all of a sudden "Neil said Tyler giggled touching Neils face they kissed Tyler unzipped Neil's jeans pulling them down sliding his hand inside his boxers Neil groaned while Tyler kissed his neck while he stroked his cock Neil hummed that feels good Neil thought while Tyler kissed his neck and ear Neil was so hard it hurt .groaning and humming they had to take it slow Neil thought while they kissed chasing each other's tongues .

TYLER BENT DOWN KISSING licking all the way down. Neil held onto his head leaning against the bed. That's good. Neil thought Tyler was sucking on him.he didn't want to come yet . " Ty not yet " Tyler stood up Neil crawled up the bed he turned to face Tyler who stripped getting onto the bed . Tyler wrapped his arms round Neil.kissed his neck his cock hard against him grinding into each other the friction making them more harder .And wet at the tips Tyler holding onto Neil.

Tyler licked and kissed down Neils back tingles all down his back he groaned, enjoying the pleasure he squirted some lube onto his fingers licking Neil's neck flipping two fingers into his entrance. Neil arched off the intrusion it was good Tyler flicking his finger in and out Neil arching up again while he stroked himself Neil turned his head and kissed Tyler he licked Neils ear nibbling at his ear .

NEIL LAY ON HIS SIDE Tyler inside him his arms wrapped around him getting into a rhythm they kissed Tyler moved Neil onto his back one leg up entering him again his face flushed Neil screamed Tyler kissing him to stifle his scream while he moved inside him Neil's face was flushed which was good to see Tyler thought .The sight off him Neil's face flushed Tyler pleasuring him he so loved him all over again .

Tyler moved Neil round onto his side sliding his arm around him guiding himself inside Neil again Tyler taking it slower he lightly slapped Neil's bottom nibbling on his shoulder leaving a slight love bite there nibbled Neil's ear he moaned again wiggling his bottom. " No teasing mister " Tyler whispered to Neil nibbling at his ear again .

They both came on a shout and collapsed onto the bed. Both sweaty Tyler moved over to Neil " I can't feel my legs' ' Neil said laughing leaning his head on Tylers shoulder Tyler kissed his head . " Happy " Neil looked up at Tyler, yes happy he thought sighing he hummed his answer . Happiest he has been in a long time Neil thought now that he has met Tyler who would have thought he would have been so understanding with his issues.

And Neil falling in love for the first time it just felt right Neil snuggled into Tyler he kissed Neil's head he was sleepy now " Wanna go again " Tyler whispers Neil looks up at him grinning " What do you think " .

JANET AND PHOEBE WE'RE closing up the shop locking the door for the night Phoebe looked round at one the regulars that recently came into the Coffee shop looked like he had been rushing " Oh your closed " Janet looked round Phoebe was blushing yes he's handsome Janet thought " Finishing up early tonight Luke ." Phoebe smiled at him while she set up the chairs on the tables.

" That's fine I can get my coffee fix someone where else " " Costa " Phoebe announces looking at Janet and back at Luke " Thanks " Lucien smiled then Roy came out he had just tidied up and they were sorting out the keys Phoebe turned round to Lucien she was going to walk with him to Costa .

" Walk with you to the bus stop " Darren asked Phoebe they said good night and both walked in the direction of the bus stop " Takevaway tonight love " Janet looked at Roy and nodded no cooking tonight she thought holding onto Roys arm walking along the road to the local takeaway which was just across the street .Being in the coffe shop all day was exhausting at times but they loved there little coffee shop and wouldn't change it .

Lucien watching them all walk along the road from the lane he stuck his hands in his pockets, a tingle sensation going through him he looked up at the sky shaking his head . " Ok I'm on my way " . Lucien sighed, shaking his head, still watching the others walk along the street . Lucien smiled. They were a good bunch. He thought he liked going into their coffee shop. It was homely .

" TYLER , TYLER" NEIL shouted from the lounge Tyler sprinted out of bed what the hell had happened rushing into the lounge Neil at the fish tank he pointed to it Tyler came over and there they were Angels baby's all five off them " Oh wow " " I know right " amazing Tyler thought they were all swimming around Angel making sure they were ok . Tyler thought Loki and Thor weren't sure of the little ones. Tyler lay his arm round Neil and they looked at each other . Then Tyler realised he had no underwear on and Neil sniggered " C'mon you let's get back to bed " " Will they be ok " Neil asked looking at the tank again he hoped so .

" Yes babe they will be ok " Good Neil thought wrapping his arms around Tyler giving him a peck on his cheek " Let's go back to bed " Tyler smiled I like that idea very much he thought slapping Neil's bottom he yelped taking his hand leading him to the bedroom for another make out session giggling on there way back into the bedroom .

TWO DAYS LATER NEIL and Tyler eventually got out of the house. They only got up to eat, shower , feed the fish and stay in bed most the day watching films in bed making out till they both got exhausted by their sex Marathon they couldn't keep their hands off each other the last two days .But who cared they thought they had making up to do and Neil had to catch up on his BL shows and there was a lot to catch up on he even got Tyler hooked on the Korean , Japanese and Chinese shows also .Just the Thai ones next Neil thought some them were good some favourites .

AS FOR DARIAN HE WAS diagnosed with Mild Reflux which he wasn't too pleased about Dr Carter told him to slow down and try not to stress too much did he listen to him no .Darian was worried about nothing down to his age but that won't stop him he thought even Malcolm and Cameron tried to convince him to so they decided to take a family Vacation to Italy to visit family much to Cameron and Malcolms delight .

Darian was more relaxed on holiday; the family gushed over baby Philip when visiting his cousins and great niece Carla in another part of Italy Santorini afterwards they drove along the coast and stayed in an apartment in Altamore overlooking the sea it was a part of Italy that Darian had wanted to take the family to which he had visited several times visiting more family there .

One of Darians distant cousins has a restaurant there Cameron and Malcolm thought it was an amazing place and vowed to come back to the place someday in the future for definite .

The End
Neil and Tyler will Return
The Little Coffee Shop On The Corner
Vol 1

BONUS CHAPTER

CHRISTMAS

CAMERON , DARIAN AND Malcolm walked down the stairs with Philip holding Malcolm's hand it was Christmas morning Philips first Christmas last night the three of them made makeshift snow sprinkling some at the bottom of the stairs on the stairs with an elf with a letter at the foot of the stairs and a little makeshift elf door . The four of them sat at the foot of the steps opening up the letter Philip sitting on Darians knee now that Philip is a year old and able to enjoy Christmas at his age .He had constantly asked for Santa for days now which Darian got annoyed about thats what its all about Malcolm had said the kids love Christmas and there will be more of them in the years to come .

" Hello " Sam shouted coming through the patio door, Frank barking, jumping up at him and Geraint. They all agreed to spend Christmas morning together before Sam and Geraint went to Geraint's parents for the rest of the day and they would open the presents and have breakfast together . The rest of them were still sitting on the stairs with Philip reading Santa's letter .

" Merry Christmas' ' Cameron said Geraint lay his arm around Sam and saw the makeshift snow very ingeniously. He thought " Santa' ' Philip shouted pointing to the lounge door . Malcolm got up taking Philip's hand "will l see if Santa has been there yet " .

Malcolm opened the door to presents in different corners of the room Philip bigger bundle " This one has been up since 5 " Darian announces yawning Malcolm sniggers Cameron lays his arm round Darian he leans into him " it is worth it to see his first Christmas " Philip toddles over to the presents Malcolm following him . " Give these to Uncle Sam and Uncle Geraint ok "

Sam and Geraint go over to Philip and Malcolm them handing them there present " Santa " Philip said again Sam and Geraint looked at each other " Did Santa come here to " Sam asked Philip looked round at Malcolm he nodded at him Philip toddled over to Sam and Geraint wanting to help open their presents also .

They opened them up a jumper each for Sam and Geraint and another present off a photo shoot Darian and the others got done with Philip " Dada " " Wow that's amazing what about these ones Philip "

Darian and Cameron watched on also helping with the old present they would eventually get to there's when Philip is finished opening his Darian looked over at Cameron the od time he looked sad Darian took his hand Cameron looked round at him " Just wish Dad was here to see him open his presents " " I know but we will talk to him later " .

Cameron's phone rang on facetime from Steven and Jordan. They had decided to go to Spain for Christmas this year. They had left presents for everyone before they left .They wished everyone a merry Christmas. Philip waved and showed off his presents to his other uncles shouting Santa Malcolm sniggered this boy has been excited the past week .

DARIAN , CAMERON AND Malcolm exchanged their presents for each other Darian had bought them each a new watch which they were both grateful for and it had better not have been expensive Malcolm thought . Malcolm got tickets for Pink's concert. He hugged Darian and Cameron for getting them; they also got the tickets for Sam and Geraint so all of them could go together .

Malcolm also got them afternoon tea and champagne he and Sam pitched in for the Red bus bistro which had been advertised on the tv and he thought it would be a good idea and it travels around Edinburgh having the afternoon tea ..

Geraint also got him and Sam Iron Maiden tickets since they both liked the band they both bonded on when they first went together and other tastes in music too8 .

Nathan called on facetime because of the time difference in Australia they had their Christmas dinner already. " Papa Papa " Cameron sat Philip on his knee while they chatted " Hello my boy was Santa good to you " Philip stuck his thumb in his mouth looking round at his dad. Cameron thought . " Tell Papa what you got " Philip hugged his dad. Yep Cameron thought he was tired holding his snuggie too .

MALCOLM AND DARIAN cleared up while Cameron chatted to his dad. Malcolm and Darian chatted to Nathan when Aida had called to say she was spending Christmas with Esther and Paula in Spain and a few friends also and they would be spending New Years with to .

LATER ON THAT DAY AFTER dinner They decided to drive to the park to take Frank with them so he can have a run around and Philip to have fresh air. Frank panted and wagged his tail excitedly because he knew where they were going . Panting in Darians ear while driving Philip chatting in his own little language but is starting to say sentences now . Waving his Transformer around Cameron tickling him " Dada no " Malcolm looks round at Philip giggling . Cameron tickled him and gave Philip a kiss as Philip giggled.

CAMERON WALKED AROUND with Frank while Malcolm and Darian sat on the bench with Philip taking photos pulling silly faces. Eventually Frank did a pee and other dog walkers were around so Frank sniffed around more while walking along the grass . Cameron looked twice and noticed someone was Hugh he thought with a dog and another guy Hugh looked up and spotted Cameron wow what a coincidence he thought Cameron coming over to him .

" Well isn't this a surprise? Cameron said as they hugged " my god yes how are you? Hugh asked, looking between Cameron and his boyfriend.

The other dog sniffing at Cameron's feet and going over to Frank " Good this is Frank " " Baxter my sisters and that's Henry " Hugh pointing to the guy with the other dog Cameron looked over at Darian and Malcolm he smiled " That's Darian and Malcolm also Philip our son "

Hugh looks at Cameron and over at the others " Philip from a surrogate " " Amazing so all three of you " Cameron nodded and grinned looking over at the others again " Yep we're in a committed throuple " Cameron held up his hand showing off his ring " .Hugh looking at it that's great to know Hugh thought and it was nice to see Cameron again after all this time .

" Hello " Hugh looks at Henry and introduces Cameron to Henry. It sounded like a New Zealand accent. Cameron thought " The writer " Henry asked, shaking hands `` That's me " while they walked over to Darian and Malcolm Cameron introducing themselves. Them and Philip " Aren't you cute " Henry said, bending down to Philip.`` He knows it too " Malcolm exclaimed Darian slid his arm around Cameron as he looked at him while chatting to Hugh and Henry .

Hugh explains he will be moving to New Zealand permanently. He and Henry were moving into a new place when they got back and planning a wedding. Cameron was pleased to hear his news . Afterwards they said their goodbyes and they went their separate ways onto the car Philip fell asleep on the way home Malcolm sat forward on the back seat .

" So that's Hugh then " grinning Darian glared in the mirror while driving Cameron looked round " Cameron looks at Darian " Not bad looking " Darian coughed seriously Malcolm thought relax shaking his head . " Not bad " Cameron said looking at Darian he looks at Cameron " But not as good looking as you and you " Cameron pinches Malcolm face . Darian smirks when Cameron notices he has the green eyed monster Cameron thinks .

THEY GOT HOME MALCOLM took Philip upstairs to have his bath while Cameron tended to Frank drying him off Darian hoovered in the kitchen Cameron looked up at him what's up with him he thought going into the fridge for wine " I'll have one to " going over to Darian taking the glass . " What are you thinking about " Darian looks up at Cameron standing in front of him " To think that time " .

Cameron put down his glass wrapping his arms round Darian " Darian that's the past ok we're looking into the future look what we have achieved the past year half ,it was weird seeing Hugh but he was just a holiday fling " .

Darian hummed touching Cameron's face, they kissed " I love you " he said " Love you more " and hugged he's thinking about Julius Cameron though Darian sat in the stool Cameron leaned against the counter . " I just wish sometimes I could have helped him more" " I know " .

" Here we are all squeaky clean " Malcolm announced coming into the kitchen swing Darian and Cameron looking serious. He's been thinking about Julius again Malcolm thought coming over to them Philip laying his arms out to Darian he took him . " oh your new "Malcolm lay his arm round Darian laying his head on his shoulder .

" Let's not be doom and gloom ok " " " we're not just a sad time with family not here " Malcolm nodded true he thought thinking about his parents to " right Dr who is on soon c'mon little man let's get your bottle " Malcolm picked up Philip going into the fridge to get his milk and they all went into the lounge to watch the Christmas special episode of Dr who . Malcolm was determined for Philip to get hooked on it just like he was .

AFTER PUTTING PHILIP to bed there was a debate on who was the best doctor back and forth until they decided on their favourite one. And their favourite companion to That night they made love twice each taking the lead and eventually falling asleep hugging each other .

New Year Came Darian opened the club for New Years eve till two am Ingride watched Philip Darian got a Dj and a local drag to come along Luca and Sydney came along to spend the evening and Celebrate the New year with them exchanging photos of Betsy Jean and Philip promising to meet up after Christmas. Sam and Geraint started their plans with Lauren for her to be their surrogate.

TYLER NEIL , TYLER'S friends Al , Oliver his fiance Jack Matt got out of the Taxi Neil looked up at Club Nero sign Tyler lay his arm round Neils shoulder he looked up at him . It's his first proper night out since he came out of Rehab 5 months ago even though they had been going to the pub a few times and holidays . Last time he was at the club was with Norman "What is this this place again " Al asked Neil snorted Tyler taking his hand looking at Al an S/m club Al " " for rea" Al was shocked thinking to himself he should check it out proper next time and check out how much the membership is .

That shocked him walking into the club. Nice he thought good decor to and for Neils sake Tyler asked everyone if they would be respectful of Neil with his sobriety which was fine by them. They wouldn't go overboard and be respectful of Neil and the guys were pleased that he was doing so well since rehab .

Neil was walking along the corridor arm in arm with Tyler when Norman Petrie appeared with someone Neil looked at Tyler feeling awkward but he will have to Talk to him " Neil "it's so lovely to see him Norman thought he had wondered how Neil was since rehab " Norman how are you " .

" good You " " good this is Tyler " Tyler nodded Norman looked at the other guy " you want me to wait " Tyler whisperer Neil looked round at Tyler " it's fine " Tyler left Neil and Norman walked along the corridor talking " His name is Harry we meet at a friends birthday 2 months ago " " That's great Norman " Norman was beaming he looked happy which was good Neil thought.

" How are things Norman asked? Neil looked up at Norman" "Tyler is amazing he knows about my past. I've been sober and clean for six months now "" That's good to know Neil and to have someone that understands your situation " .

" Norman the Uber will.be here soon " Harry looked between Norman and Neil he acknowledge Neil " Be there in a minute " Harry disappeared to check on the Uber " Norman about the payments you don't have to anymore I'm doing ok " Norman knew he had to talk to Neil about that sometime " I understand I will get onto that soon " .

THEY SAID THEIR GOODBYES and hugged. Norman understood what Neil meant. He patted his back wishing him well then left. Neil went through to the bar. Al was getting the drinks. Tyler lay his arm round Neil " ok " Neil nodded and they went to one the booths with the others .

" Ty " Tyler looked at Neil before they went to sit. He thought, " What's wrong? " " I'm fine . I told him about it. " Tyler knew what Neil meant. Tyler brought Neil closer to him, hugging him. Jesus Neil thought about strangling him . " What's wrong are you ok " Oliver asked looking worried Neil and Tyler looked at him looked at each other " olly its fine Neils fine " " i can talk for myself you know just family stuff "

They went over to the booth and sat Al looking round again, finding the club fascinating and noticed a cute guy over at the far side catching his attention . " So how much is the membership then? " Al asked, looking between the guys .

Everyone looked at him shaking their heads " what did i say something wrong " " No Al you didnt but he's the guy to ask " Neil pointed to Darian over at the Vip " is he the guy in the throuple cause he is hot " very hot Al thought and he could see why he had two boyfriends and they looked happy to lucky guy Al thought .

Everyone giggled, shaking their heads. " Are you Horny or just curious? " Oliver asked, not funny. He thought of taking a drink of his beer and was curious about the bar. Al thought everyone was looking at him . " What I'm only curious to know " .

LUCIEN AND JULIUS STOOD watching everyone Julius looked at Lucien and back at Darian with Cameron and Malcolm Julius smiled they looked happy that's what Julius wanted for him to be happy and not feel guilty for what happened in the past " Lucien there ok aren't they " Julius looked at Lucien he looked at Julius `` yes there ok " good Julius thought . " Lucien can I see him "looking round at Lucien " off course " .

Julius looked down at Philip asleep in his cot. This is what Darian wanted for years as a family and now his wish came true with the two men he was In love with. Julius just wished sometimes he made him happy. That's one regret . " Julius you two were happy once don't forget that " Julius looked round at Lucien yes in the beginning they were when Darian got him clean . A tingle went through Lucien Julius looks at him again " We have to go don't we " " Sorry "

JULIUS LOOKS DOWN AT Philip again " you be good for your dads little one "

MUCH LATER AFTER THE bells and everyone went home Tyler and Neil made love twice Neil on top first after Neil topped Tyler they often versed in there lovemaking and after they lay in bed snuggled into each other " Ty ' " mmm " Neil turned to face Tyler he opened his eyes to look at Neil " Al should really get a boyfriend " Tyler sniggered what's brought this on he thought. " Babe he's had plenty of boyfriends `` oh " Tyler kissed Neil's nose laying his arm around him .

" Ty " Tyler sighed opening his eyes again seriously it's four am will he stop asking questions " What " Neil lay his head on Tyler's stomach looking up at him " I love you " " Your a menace " Neil screwed up his face he reached up kissing Tyler " now go to sleep please "

AT FOUR AM DARIAN , Cameron and Malcolm eventually got home all three of them were in Philips room looking down at him watching him sleep they looked at each other arms around each other .sleep was calling them before they went to there bedroom Darian noticed something on the ground beside Philips cot . A white feather he picked up what does that mean he thought .

Cameron stood at the door watching Darian. He looked up at him. " What is it? "" A feather is strange isn't it? Darian said, holding up the feather Cameron inspecting it. Probably an eagle's feather babe, c'mon let's go to bed ."

Darian left the feather on the rocking chair. He's probably overthinking it Darian thought looking round at Philip before he left going into the bedroom taking off his jacket going into the walk-in wardrobe. To get changed thinking about the feather is a sign he thought .

Malcolm wrapped his arms around Darians waist. He turned his head to kiss him. They moved into the bedroom. All three hugged before getting into bed. They fell asleep within ten minutes exhausted from the festivities . A new year and possibly another new business Darian thought .

Cameron looked round at Darian what's he thinking about he thought laying his head on his shoulder " Darian your overthinking again " he looked down at Malcolm I'm not he thought just curious about the feather that's all Malcolm slid his hand into the covers Darian took his hand looking and grinning at Malcolm .

" See that stopped you overthinking " Darian bent to kiss him looks at Cameron all three kiss each other " I can't wait to see what the new year brings " Darian exclaims then lays down Cameron and Malcolm at each side and me to both Cameron and Malcolm thinking the same .

The End

CLUB NERO SERIES WILL Return

CLUB NERO SERIES - THE NEXT CHAPTER - VOL 4   213

His Cold Heart Series
His Cold Heart
Vol 1
Warm Heart
Vol 2
The Warmest Heart
Vol 3

Linktree
https://Linktr.ee/dalevmcfarlane[1]

G

Don't miss out!

Visit the website below and you can sign up to receive emails whenever Dale v Mcfarlane publishes a new book. There's no charge and no obligation.

https://books2read.com/r/B-A-WMJU-YKLRC

BOOKS 2 READ

Connecting independent readers to independent writers.

About the Author

Hi i am Dale i live in scotland writting is my passion i also write fan fic to please check out my socials

9 798223 622130